Against All Odds

Mario DeSean Booker

Against All Odds

Against All Odds: An Unbroken Story
Rev. Dr. Mario DeSean Booker

Against All Odds: An Unbroken Story

Dedication

*T*o Me.
You chose this.

Not the pain—God knows you didn't choose that. But you chose to open the curtain, to let someone turn on the lights in that dark room where you had buried everything. You chose to sit in Dr. Reed's chair when every survival-coded instinct told you to run. You chose to write this book when silence would have been easier, cleaner, safer.

Nobody taught you courage. They taught you compliance. They taught you smallness. They beat into you the theology of invisible boys who do not cry, do not ask, do not tell.

You chose courage anyway.

This book is not about what was done to you. It is about what you refused to let that become—the moment you stopped running from your own story and decided, with full deliberation, to write the rest of it yourself.

That took everything.

I am proud of you.

To Little Mario, born August 13, 1980, Flint, Michigan.

I see you.

Down there in that basement. Five years old, back pressed against the pole, wrists raw, listening to the floorboards above you, calculating threat by sound alone because that's what you had to learn before you learned to read. You should have been learning to ride a bike.

You were not the problem.

Not one beating, not one night chained to that pole, not one moment of your young life that smelled of mildew and blood and terror—none of it happened because you deserved it. You were a child. His brokenness was not your inheritance, even though he handed it to you like it was.

You survived on the scraps of love that filtered through, and when there were none, you survived on the spider in the window, on the sliver of sky from the basement floor, on whatever fragment of faith or pure biological will kept your heart beating.

That little boy—you—is the reason any of this is possible.

The boy chained to a pole in Flint, Michigan would one day stand in a pulpit, stand in a classroom, stand beside a woman who chose him deliberately, and hold twin sons who will never know the darkness you knew.

Rest now. I've got it from here.

To Rev. Dr. Mario DeSean Booker, Ph.D.

No one who knew that basement could have predicted you.

Not the man who holds a doctorate and teaches the next generation of scholars. Not the minister who stands before a congregation offering grace to people still trapped in their own basements. Not the husband, not the father of sons, not the author who put his own wounds on paper because he understood—the way only the healed can—that testimony is a form of medicine.

Every door closed out of politics or prejudice or plain cowardice. Every professional betrayal, every setback dressed up as a dead end. Every moment you built your credentials while someone with half your capacity had theirs handed to them—those were not obstacles to your story. They became your story. The gold in the cracks. The Kintsugi version of a man.

The Ph.D. after your name is not the miracle. The miracle is that you wanted it at all—that after everything tried to make you small, you still had the audacity to pursue the highest room in the house.

The Reverend in you knows what the Doctor can explain and what the boy in the basement already felt long before either title arrived: God was in that darkness too. Not causing it. Present in it—to ensure the vessel didn't shatter before it could be filled.

You were filled.

Go pour.

This book is written in the blood of a boy who should not have made it—and the ink of a man who refused to pretend he didn't.

—Rev. Dr. Mario DeSean Booker, Ph.D.

Acknowledgments

God **Almighty**: the only One who could take a boy chained to a basement pole and architect something this beautiful from those ruins. You did not waste one moment of my pain. Every wound became a word. Every scar became a sentence. Every night I spent invisible, You were already writing the chapter where I stood in the light. I did not always understand Your methods, but I have never doubted Your authorship. This book—this *life*—belongs to You first.

My pain: I never thought I would say this, and I mean it with everything in me: thank you. Not for what you were, but for what you made inevitable. You were the fire, and I am the gold that had no business surviving the temperature. Every breaking was a making I could not see at the time. You shaped my empathy, sharpened my theology, and gave me a story worth telling. Without you, I am ordinary. Because of you, I am *this*.

FaLessia: My wife, my editor, my person. You saw me before I fully saw myself, and you stayed anyway—through the rough drafts of this manuscript and the rougher drafts of my healing. You are the safe place I did not know I was building toward. Every page of this book passed through your hands, and so did I. I am better at both because of you. I love you beyond the margins of any page I will ever write.

To **every soul who poured into me**: The mentors who invested without guaranteed return, the church family that offered grace without a checklist, the teachers who saw potential in a boy who had learned to make himself small, the friends who stayed when staying cost something. You may not have known what you were doing in that moment. You were saving a life. You were filling a cup that had been deliberately drained for years.

Because of all of you:

My cup runneth over.—Psalm 23:5

This story was written in braille...

So you can feel it!

Loving in Shadows

When we love in secrecy.
When we love in untruth.
When we love with clothed nakedness.
When we love and die.
When the shadows of our past cloak our future.
When you've given love your all.
Then you have been "Loving in Shadows."
Mario DeSean Booker

Table of Contents

Dedication 5

Acknowledgments 7

Loving in Shadows 3

Foreword 7

Prologue 9

Chapter 1: When Love Wore the Face of Fear 13

Memory: Christmas Morning, 1984 14

Chapter 2: Loving in Shadows 21

Memory: The Book Incident 23

Chapter 3: The Whole Circus 29

Chapter 4: Walking on Broken Glass 37

Chapter 5: When Love Meant Blood 47

Memory: The Human Punching Bag 50

Chapter 6: The Crumbs They Called Love 55

Memory: Christmas Fun with Chevon 55

Memory: The House Fire 60

Chapter 7: When God and Pain Shared the Same Pew 71

Memory: Joining Church 71

Memory within a Memory...Proverbs 3:5-6 75

Back in Dr. Reed's office... 77

Chapter 8: Checkmate 79

Passing 84

Dear Seeker 87

Chapter 9: Broken Early 89

Memory: Innocence Lost 91

Chapter 10: The Deep Calls to Deep 97

Chapter 11: FEAR = False Evidence Appearing Real 105

Memory: The Millionaire's Ball 106

Fast Forward Ten Years 107

The Devastating Realization 109

Back to Reality 111

Chapter 12: When Goliath Fled 113

Memory: Mama's Missing 113

The Arrival 115

Mama's Meltdown 116

My Response 116

The Aftermath 117

Dr. Reed's Analysis 117

Chapter 13: Season of Growth 121

Two Years Later 121

The Evolution of Love 122

The Ring on the Dresser 122

Building My Empire 123

Dr. Reed's Wisdom 124

The Foundation of Everything 125

Looking Forward 125

Chapter 14: Stepping Stones 127

A Winter Wedding 127

The Children Who Grew in Our Hearts 131

Education Against All Odds 131

The Letter From Dr. Reed 133

Moving Forward 137

About the Author 139

Foreword

The trees spoke out to me today
    Like a rustle of wind spoken through the leaves
The scent of amaryllis sways in the wind
I remember our forbidden love
The shadow of our love
Haunts me without ceasing
My perdition
We loved in secrecy
Met in words
Dreamed in riddles
Kissed with fists
Loved in shadows
Hidden...Dare we not show our love.
Let us touch with gloved hands
Kiss with shielded lips
Look with blinded eyes
Let us not love...but love!
Your exodus from my world ...
Your prejudicial departure...
You being ripped from my very arms
Left me lonely.
And when they ripped you they left your shadow.
This fictitious, monochromatic entity of you.
That haunts me with memories of you

Just lies there...because of you
And now I am left here
Loving in Shadows
Without you.
Mario DeSean Booker

Prologue

I hear the floor creak.

The devil himself has taken his first steps into hell.

I gaze around the shadow, the darkness—this suffocating black void that swallows me whole. My eyes strain, pupils dilated with terror, searching for something, anything, that makes sense in this nightmare. The musty stench of mildew burns my nostrils. The acrid smell of my own dried blood mingles with the putrid odor of soiled clothes scattered like evidence of countless crimes.

Time? *What is time when you're buried alive in your own home?*

And as I move—*God, the pain*—fire shoots up my spine like lightning striking the same broken tree again and again. Every nerve ending screams. I want to move but I can't. My body is no longer mine. It belongs to him. It's another thing he breaks when he's angry.

Memories flood my mind like water releasing from a dam—no, like a tsunami of horror crashing over me, drowning me in the remembrance of what these hands have done to my small body. He did this to me and left me here. Left only with tears and darkness and pain so deep it has its own heartbeat.

Clank. Clank.

The sound echoes through the basement like chains dragging souls to damnation. As I move my hands, the metal bracelets—these aren't bracelets, they're shackles, they're ownership papers written in steel—make a sound that announces my captivity to the darkness itself.

Symbol of love? No. Symbol of possession. Of power. Of a monster marking his territory.

And as consciousness crawls back into my shattered world, the truth hits me like another blow to the face: I am chained to a pole in the basement again.

Tears flood and streak my face as I remember the beating. The breaking of flesh. The searing pain of the extension cord as it wraps around my body. I remember the look of my abuser's face. Combined in that face was, to my mind, the epitome of evil. There was a hint of joy that I could envision on his face. Almost like a maestro in an orchestra, conducting—with every stroke of that cord, I screamed louder and louder.

It wasn't necessarily a scream of pain, but rather, if I scream loud enough, maybe someone will hear me. Maybe someone will see me. I often felt invisible except when I was needed to be a punching bag.

This room stinks. Mildew. Soiled clothes scattered about. Dark and rank. *Was I going to die here?*

I look around as my eyes begin to adjust to the smothering darkness. I sat there—no hope of a savior, clinging to fear that another round was coming. I hear them upstairs. To an untrained ear and eye, they look and sound like a perfect family. They didn't need me. Hence why I'm down here.

I peer through the window and can discern a spider crawling around in his web. *Oh, how I envied him.* His freedom. The ability of the spider to craft his own world, to be ruthless, to have solace, to have freedom.

I clank the chains more, not sure why I was handcuffed to this pole. There's no way I can break free.

Clank. Clank. Clank. Clank.

I hear more creaks. I look up to the ceiling and hear footsteps. Fear grabs and takes hold of me. Oh, dear friend, I would like to say that I missed you, but me and fear have become so synonymous together. Like sugar and Kool-Aid, like peanut butter and jelly—a oneness I have become with fear. The moment I can exist without fear is a moment in which I will be waiting for pain.

Some will say this was sad, even unfathomable, but this was my world. We existed together, both I and fear.

I hear footsteps coming down the stairs. My heart does flips in my chest. I scurry around the pole, turning my bruised back positioned against the wall. I need to see who's coming. I need to prepare for what's about to happen. I don't know what's coming, but it's never good. Although I cannot change this, I need to prepare myself for the inevitable.

I squint my eyes in the darkness to see the silhouette of a large figure. Suddenly the lights flash on, and through my blindness, I try to discern who is in front of me. Still not able to see clearly, not willing to let my guard down, I cover my face and, as if I was set on autoplay, I started to cry.

"You still crying?"

That unmistakable voice. Although I could not see clearly, I knew exactly who it was. It was the monster.

Now, even as a child, we are all taught about monsters. Big, ugly, alien-like beings who come to do us harm. But we're never told or shown what a true monster looks like. They are not like the movies or the comic books. They walk with us, they talk with us, they live with us, they breathe with us, and in some cases, they even give birth to us.

"No sir," I struggle to say.

However, my eyes betray me. I gotta get it together. If I continue to cry, more of the same is coming. *Come on, Mario, get it together. Be strong. You got this. This isn't the first time, and it's not going to be the last time. Push through.*

I struggle with chained hands to clear my face. I try to stand but fall back down. Searing pain comes from my legs. I look down to see blood splatters on the ground, and I'm able to contort my body to look at my legs and see that they are covered with welts. So it wasn't just my back.

I raise my head and look at the monster in his eyes. My friend comes back to me—fear. Fear so strong that I almost urinated at the sight of this demon. I shake so hard internally that my teeth start to chatter.

"I'm sick of your shit," the monster spews venomously.

"Yes sir, I just—"

"You just *what*?" He challenges as he steps forward toward me. I shrink back, forgetting my place.

Sigh. Mario, you know better. You don't speak back. You want another one? Is this what you really want? Just fall in line.

"No sir," I replied. This response seems to satiate the monster. This is what I would do then.

Five years old. This is what I knew. This is what love looked like in my world. This is what happens when monsters wear the face of fathers and houses become concentration camps and childhood becomes a death sentence you serve one beating at a time.

"Mario... Mario... I'm going to count backwards from 5. When we get to 1, you'll be back in my office. 5... 4... 3... 2... 1..."

SNAP!

My eyes explode, opening like gunshots in the dark.

Where am I? WHERE AM I?

My heart hammers against my ribcage like a caged animal desperate for freedom. Sweat pours down my face in rivers of terror. My hands fly to my wrists—no chains. NO CHAINS. But phantom pain burns where metal once bit into flesh. My breath comes in ragged gasps, hyperventilating, drowning in air that tastes like freedom but feels like a lie.

This room—bright, clean, safe—it's wrong, it's all wrong. Where are the shadows? Where is the stench? Where is the monster?

I see her. A middle-aged woman sitting in a chair with a pen and notepad, taking notes like she's documenting the destruction of my soul. Did I tell her? WHAT DID I TELL HER? The panic rises in my throat like bile. I was never supposed to tell anybody what happened. *Never.* NEVER. The first rule of survival: secrets keep you alive, truth gets you killed.

I would get a beating—or get killed—if I told anyone.

The room spins. Reality fractures. Past and present collide like freight trains in my mind.

I burst from the chair, tears streaming, body moving on pure survival instinct, rushing toward the door like my life depends on it because my life HAS always depended on running, hiding, escaping, surviving—

She stops me.

"Mario, you're okay. Come here. You're safe."

Safe? SAFE? That word doesn't exist in my vocabulary. That word is a fairytale. That word is a lie people tell children before they hurt them.

"What you just experienced was a regression to one of the many traumatic points in your life. I took you to that place so we can examine why you are—or rather who you are—today. No one's going to harm you. You're not that little boy anymore, and the monster isn't here."

The "monster."

She knows.

She KNOWS.

But when I look around—really look—she's right. I'm not five years old. These hands are man-sized. This body has grown beyond the reach of his fists. I'm not that little kid anymore. I'm a grown man who chose to walk into this office, who chose to face the demons, who chose to remember instead of running.

Memories flood back, dawn breaking through an endless night. I see and remember that I am here to get help. She's right—I am safe. For the first time in my life, I am actually, *truly* safe.

A smile breaks across my face like sunrise after the longest winter of my soul. *Yes, I am free. Yes, I am safe. Yes, I survived.*

"I think that's enough for today, but I do want to see you regularly. We have so much exploration to do and so much healing that needs to happen. Together, we will get you through this."

"Thanks, Dr. Reed."

I realize this is going to be a journey—my healing journey. It's time for me to look under the rocks. It's time to open up the curtains and let the light in. I was told never to discuss our business, but this is *my* business now. And in order for me to grow, I have to let go of that which is holding me back.

This is my story.

Not only of that five-year-old boy—broken, bleeding, chained like an animal in the depths of hell itself.

Not only of survival—because surviving is what animals do, what the desperate do, what those without choice must do.

This is the story of a man who looked into the eyes of his demons and said, "No more."

A man who took those very chains that bound him and forged them into wings.

A man who chose to transform his scars into stars, his wounds into wisdom, his pain into purpose.

You see, every phoenix must first burn. Must feel the searing flames consume everything they once were. Must turn to ash, must become nothing, must face the terrifying possibility that the fire will be their end.

But here's what they don't tell you about phoenixes:

The burning? That's not the miracle.

The rising? That's not the miracle either.

The miracle is the choice.

The choice to believe that you are more than your ashes.

The choice to spread wings you cannot yet see.

The choice to fly when everything in you screams to stay buried in the safety of the ground.

Every phoenix must first burn.

But every phoenix—every single one—chooses to fly.

This is how I chose to soar.

Chapter 1: When Love Wore the Face of Fear

I pace across Dr. Reed's office like a caged animal. Back and forth, back and forth. My feet trace the same path in her carpet that I've worn smooth over these past few weeks. The leather chair that holds so many of my secrets sits empty, mocking me.

"Mario, please sit down. You're safe here."

Safe. That word again. The word that feels foreign on my tongue, impossible in my world.

"I don't know if I can do this again, Doc." My voice cracks like I'm still that little boy. "Last session... going back there... It's messed me up for days. I keep waking up thinking I'm back in that basement."

Dr. Reed's eyes soften with understanding. She's seen this before—patients standing at the edge of their own healing, terrified to jump. "I know it's difficult, Mario. But running from these memories gives them power over you. We need to take that power back."

I finally slump into the chair, exhausted from fighting myself. "But it's all bad. Every memory I have is just... pain. Violence. Fear. How is reliving that supposed to help me?"

"Not every memory is wrapped in trauma, Mario. Sometimes the mind buries the good ones deepest, to protect them from the pain that follows." She leans forward, her voice gentle but insistent. "Today, I want to try something different. Instead of me taking you back to a traumatic moment, I want you to search for something else. A fond memory. A moment of joy."

I laugh, but there's no humor in it. "Doc, I don't think you understand. There weren't any. My childhood was one long nightmare."

"I believe there were moments of light, even in your darkness. Sometimes they're hidden beneath layers of hurt." She gestures toward the couch. "Will you lie down? Let me guide you through a meditation. Let your mind wander freely. Don't force it. Just... let yourself remember."

Reluctantly, I move to the couch. The leather is cool against my back as I close my eyes. Dr. Reed's voice becomes a distant anchor as she guides me into relaxation, asking me to breathe deeply, to let my mind drift backward through time.

"Don't search for anything specific, Mario. Just let your consciousness float. What comes up?"

At first, there's only darkness. The familiar black void of suppressed memories—a psychological fortress my mind constructed to protect itself. Dr. Reed explained this phenomenon to me before: when trauma becomes too overwhelming, the psyche creates these empty spaces, these neural dead zones where memories go to hide. It's not that the memories don't exist; they're buried beneath layers of psychological concrete, sealed away like toxic waste.

The void isn't empty, though. It pulses with the weight of everything I've forgotten, everything I've forced myself not to remember. It's alive with the echoes of screams that were silenced, tears that were forbidden, words that were swallowed before they could escape. The blackness is thick, suffocating, like being underwater in an ocean of suppressed pain.

My mind resists, throwing up walls, sending signals of danger. *Don't go there. Don't remember. Forgetting is survival. Remembering is death.*

But Dr. Reed's voice cuts through the psychological static: "Mario, I want you to remember something. The Bible tells us that weeping may endure for a night, but joy comes in the morning. Your night has been long, son, but morning is coming. Let the light of truth shine into that darkness."

Her words feel like a lifeline thrown into the abyss. I grab hold, letting her faith become a bridge over my fear.

"The Scripture also says that all things work together for good to those who love God. Even this darkness, Mario. Even these memories you're afraid of. God can use them for your healing, for your purpose. Trust Him. Trust the process."

And slowly, like dawn breaking through storm clouds, something emerges from the psychological wasteland.

Memory: Christmas Morning, 1984

I am four years old.

The smell hits me first—a symphony of soul food aromas that makes my stomach growl with anticipation. Mama's in the kitchen, and the whole house smells like Heaven. The rich, smoky scent of ham mingles with the earthy aroma of collard greens. I can hear the sizzle of chicken frying, imagine the bubbling of mac and cheese in the oven.

"Michael! Mario! Y'all come eat!" Mama calls from the kitchen, her voice warm and musical.

My brother and I race through the house, sliding on the hardwood floors in our sock feet. The Christmas tree towers in the corner of the living room, its branches heavy with ornaments and nearly buried beneath a mountain of wrapped presents. The colored lights blink in patterns that hypnotize me, casting rainbow shadows on the walls.

"Slow down in there!" Mama hollers, but I can hear the smile in her voice.

The dining room table groans under the weight of Christmas dinner. Cornbread dressing golden and crispy on top. Collard greens glistening with ham fat. Mac and cheese so rich and creamy it looks like liquid gold. Sweet potato pie cooling on the counter. Her famous sweet potato—the one that made people beg for the recipe she'd never give up. Potato salad creamy and perfect, dotted with paprika. Everything made from scratch, made with love.

Mama moves through the kitchen like a conductor orchestrating a symphony. Her hair is done up nice, and she's wearing her good dress—the red one with tiny flowers that she saves for special occasions. She hums while she works, occasionally breaking into full song when her favorite Christmas carol comes on the radio.

"Y'all better wash them hands before you touch my food," she says, pointing a wooden spoon at us with mock sternness.

From his recliner in the living room, Senior watches TV, but I can see his eyes tracking us as we run around. He's dressed nice too—clean shirt, pants with a crease. He's got his glass, ice clinking against crystal, dark liquor catching the Christmas lights, and every now and then he calls out to Mama about how good everything smells.

For this moment, we look like what families are supposed to look like. We sound like joy.

"Mario, come help Mama carry this," she says, handing me the basket of cornbread. I beam with pride at being trusted with something so important.

"We gonna eat all this food before we go to Grandma Booker's house?" I ask.

Mama's face shifts slightly—a shadow crossing the sun. "Mike wants food here for later. We'll eat some now, then eat the rest later if we're hungry when we come back."

I nod, not understanding the undercurrent of tension in her voice. All I know is that we're about to eat like kings, and then we get to go see Grandma and Grandpa Booker, and Christmas doesn't get much better than that.

"Mama, why don't we take some of this good food to Grandma's house?" I ask innocently.

The wooden spoon freezes in her hand. From the living room, Senior 's voice cuts through the Christmas music: "What he say?"

Mama's eyes darted between the kitchen doorway and my confused face. "Nothing, Mike. The boy was asking about dinner."

But I see it now—the way her shoulders tense, the way her hands tremble slightly as she stirs the greens. The way she glances toward the living room like she's calculating distances and escape routes.

"Your mama's food ain't welcomed at my mama's house," Senior calls out, and there's an edge to his voice that makes my stomach twist. "She knows that. Don't you, Jean?"

I don't understand why taking food to Grandma's would be bad, but I sense the danger lurking beneath the surface of our perfect Christmas morning. Mama and Grandma Booker—their relationship is complicated in ways my four-year-old mind can't grasp. It's all silent feuds and passive-aggressive comments and unspoken rules about respect and territory.

The festivities continue, but now there's a current of electricity in the air. Senior 's glass drains and refills, drains and refills. His laughter gets louder, his comments sharper. Mama moves more carefully, speaks more softly, like she's walking through a minefield.

I'm helping carry dishes to the table when it happens.

The glass dish slips from Mama's hands like it's coated in grease. Time slows as I watch it fall—the ceramic dish filled with golden mac and cheese, Senior 's favorite, tumbling through the air before exploding against the kitchen floor in a symphony of shattered glass and scattered food.

The silence that follows is deafening.

"JEAN! What the hell is wrong with you?"

Senior 's voice booms from the living room, and Mama's face goes pale. I freeze in the doorway, the basket of cornbread trembling in my small hands.

"I'm sorry, Mike. I'm sorry. Let me clean it up."

But he's already in the kitchen, towering over her, his face twisted with rage. "You can't do nothing right, can you? Nothing! I ask for one thing—one damn thing—and you can't even hold a dish!"

"Mike, please. The boys—"

"Don't you dare tell me about the boys when you're the one messing up Christmas!"

Mama backs toward the stove where the cast iron skillet sits, still hot from frying chicken. Grease pops and sizzles. Her hand hovers near the handle, and for a moment, her eyes flash with something dangerous.

"You put your hands on me again, Mike Booker, and I swear I'll throw this hot grease all over you."

The threat hangs in the air like smoke. For a heartbeat, I think maybe Mama has found her power, maybe she's going to protect herself, protect us.

Then I hear it.

SMACK!

The sound of his hand connecting with her face echoes through the kitchen like a gunshot. Mama staggers backward, her hand flying to her cheek. The skillet clatters as she grabs the counter for support.

"MAMA!"

The word tears from my throat before I can stop it. I drop the corn-bread and rush toward the kitchen, but everything happens so fast. Senior. whips around, his eyes finding me, and suddenly he's charging like a bull seeing red.

"MAMA!" I scream again, but she's already moving, throwing herself between us.

"Don't you touch him! Please, Mike, don't touch my baby!"

Her hands press against his chest, and for a moment they struggle, her small frame against his bulk. He grabs her shirt, lifting her slightly off her feet, his face inches from hers.

"You better teach that boy to mind his own business," he snarls.

Then he releases her, shoving her backward. She catches herself against the counter, breathing hard. He grabs a dish towel from the rack and throws it at her feet.

"Clean up this mess and get ready to go. We're already late."

As he storms past me, his shoulder slams into mine, sending me sprawling against the wall. Stars explode behind my eyes, but I don't cry. I've learned not to cry in front of him.

Mama kneels on the floor, picking up pieces of broken glass with shaking hands. Mac and cheese clings to her good dress, staining the tiny flowers. I want to help her, but my body won't move. I'm frozen against the wall, watching my mother clean up the evidence of her humiliation.

"Come on, baby," she whispers to me as she stands. "Help Mama finish getting ready."

She changes clothes in silence, her movements mechanical. When she emerges from the bedroom, she's put on makeup to cover the red mark on her cheek, but I can still see it underneath the powder.

The ride to Grandma Booker's house is a tomb of silence. Michael Junior and I sit in the back seat, staring out our respective windows. Mama stares straight ahead, her hands folded in her lap. Senior drives with one hand, the radio playing Christmas carols that mock us with their joy.

As we pull into Grandma's driveway, Senior turns around to face us. His eyes are cold, calculating.

"Y'all listen to me and listen good. What happens in our house stays in our house. Family business is family business. If anybody asks you anything—anybody—you tell them everything's fine. You understand me?"

Michael Junior nods quickly. I stare.

"I said, do you understand me, boy?"

"Yes sir," I whisper.

"Because if I find out one of y'all ran your mouth about our business, I'll kill you. You hear me? I'll kill all of you."

The garage door opens, and suddenly we're expected to transform. Like actors stepping onto a stage, we arrange our faces into masks of Christmas happiness.

Grandma and Grandpa Booker emerge from the house, arms outstretched, voices filled with holiday cheer. "Merry Christmas! Come here and give us some sugar!"

On cue, we smile. We hug. We perform the ritual of family joy.

But I'm not good at acting. I'm four years old, and my face is an open book written in a language of confusion and fear.

Grandma Booker's eyes find mine immediately. She sees past the forced smile, past the careful choreography of our arrival. Her weathered hands cup my face as she kneels down to my level.

"What's wrong with Granny's baby?" she asks softly.

Over her shoulder, I see Senior 's face. His expression is a mixture of rage and warning, a look that dares me to defy his orders. A look that promises consequences if I speak the truth.

Michael Junior nudges me with his elbow—a silent reminder of the rules, of what happens to little boys who tell family business to outsiders.

My eyes dart between Grandma's concerned face and Senior 's threatening glare, then to Mama, who stands behind him. Her face is a desperate plea wrapped in fear. Don't upset the natural order, her eyes beg. Don't make it worse than it already is. Accept the status quo. Survive.

Fear wins.

"I'm okay, Granny," I lie, my voice barely above a whisper.

She studies my face for a long moment, and I know she doesn't believe me. But she also knows not to push, not with Senior standing right there, not with the unspoken rules that govern our family's dysfunction.

This is the first time I can recall responding with fear instead of truth. But even as the memory crystallizes in my four-year-old mind, I know with terrible certainty that this is not the first time.

This is the first time I remember choosing silence over safety, lies over liberation.

The first time I remember learning that truth is dangerous, and that love means protecting the people who hurt you.

My eyes snap open in Dr. Reed's office. My face is wet with tears I don't remember shedding.

"Mario? You're back. How do you feel?"

I sit up slowly, wiping my eyes, but anger is building inside me like steam in a kettle. "I thought...I thought it was a good memory. Christmas morning, Mama cooking, the tree full of presents. But even that..." My voice breaks, then hardens. "Even the good memories are poisoned."

Dr. Reed nods knowingly. "But did you notice something important in that memory, Mario?"

I shake my head, confused, but the anger is growing stronger.

"Your mother fought for you. She threw herself between you and danger. And your grandmother—she saw. She knew something was wrong. Even in that house of fear, there were people who loved you, who wanted to protect you."

"PROTECT ME?" The words explode from my mouth before I can stop them. I jumped up from the couch, pacing again, but this time it's not anxiety—it's rage. "If Granny knew, then the family knew! And nobody stepped in! Nobody protected us—nobody protected ME!"

My voice cracks with decades of suppressed fury. "You want to talk about my grandmother seeing? She SAW and did nothing! She SAW and let us go back home with that monster! She SAW and chose to keep the family peace instead of protecting a four-year-old boy!"

I'm shouting now, tears streaming down my face. "I lived unprotected, Dr. Reed! UNPROTECTED! While adults who claimed to love me watched me disappear into that house of horrors and did NOTHING!"

The silence in the room is deafening. Dr. Reed sits quietly, letting my rage fill the space between us.

"You're right, Mario," she says softly. "You did live unprotected. And that little boy deserved so much more than the silence of people who saw but didn't act."

For the first time, I saw it. Buried beneath the trauma and terror, there were seeds of love. Imperfect, complicated, dangerous love—but love nonetheless. But love that sees but doesn't act is another form of abandonment.

"The memory isn't about the violence, Mario. It's also about the love that existed alongside it. The love that tried to shield you, even when it couldn't stop the pain. But you're also right—it's about the love that failed you. The protection that should have been there but wasn't."

I lean back against the couch, exhausted from the emotional eruption, but somehow the anger has cleared something inside me. "What now, Doc? How do I forgive people who saw me drowning and threw me thoughts and prayers instead of a life preserver?"

"Now we keep digging. We find more of those seeds of love, and we learn the difference between the love that protected you and the fear that silenced you. Because that little boy who chose silence? He was trying to survive. But the man sitting here with me today? He gets to choose truth."

She leans forward, her voice taking on the cadence of someone who's walked through fire herself. "Mario, the Bible says that the truth shall set you free. But what it doesn't tell you is that first, the truth will make you miserable. It will drag you through every dark valley, every shadow of death. But weeping may endure for a night—your night has been long, son—but joy comes in the morning."

She pauses, letting the words sink in like seeds in fertile soil.

"And here's what I know about God's plan for your life: Romans 8:28 tells us that all things work together for good to those who love God, to those who are the called according to His purpose. Even this pain, Mario. Even that basement. Even that Christmas when love wore the face of fear. God is going to use every broken piece of your story to build something beautiful."

I feel something shift inside me—a crack in the wall I've built around my heart.

"You were fearfully and wonderfully made, Mario. Not despite your scars but including them. David knew about darkness too. He wrote, 'Yea, though I walk through the valley of the shadow of death, I will fear no evil.' Notice he didn't say 'if' he walked through the valley—he said 'though.' He knew the valley was part of the journey to the mountain-top."

For the first time since I've been coming to therapy, I don't just believe her—I feel it in my bones. There's a stirring in my spirit, a whisper that says maybe this pain has a purpose.

Maybe there is a way out of this darkness after all.

Chapter 2: Loving in Shadows

I arrive at Dr. Reed's office carrying the weight of another sleepless night. The Unrequited Lover's rejection still burns fresh in my chest—dismissing my plea to make our relationship public, showing cold indifference to my desperate need to be chosen, to be claimed, to be worthy of someone's open affection.

The Unrequited Lover. Even the name I've given this person tells the whole story, doesn't it? For months, I've been caught in a web of half-promises and midnight confessions, stolen moments that felt like everything and nothing all at once. I would get texts at 2 AM, vulnerable and needy words pouring out about loneliness and connection. But come daylight, I became a dirty little secret again.

"I care about you, Mario," would come whispered in the darkness of that apartment, "but you have to understand my position. I can't be seen with you. People wouldn't understand."

People wouldn't understand. As if love was something to be ashamed of. As if *I* was something to be ashamed of.

Last night was supposed to be different. We went to dinner at a quiet restaurant across town—far enough away that the Unrequited Lover felt safe from prying eyes. I'd rehearsed my speech for weeks, the words I thought would finally convince this person to step into the light with me.

"I love you," I said, reaching across the table. "I'm tired of hiding. I'm tired of pretending we're friends when people ask. I want to be yours, publicly, proudly."

The way my hand was pulled away was like a physical blow. "Mario, we've talked about this. You know I can't. My family, my job, my reputation—there's too much at stake."

"What about *my* heart?" I asked, my voice breaking in that restaurant. "What about what's at stake for me?"

The look I received was something that might have been pity. "You're being dramatic. What we have is special because it's private. Why do you need everyone else's validation?"

Because I've spent my whole life being someone's secret shame, I wanted to scream. *Because I've been hidden away in basements and silenced with threats and made to feel like my very existence was something to be ashamed of.*

But I didn't say that. I sat there, watching the person I loved reduce my need for dignity to "being dramatic."

The Unrequited Lover paid the check—always insisting on paying, as if money could somehow balance the scales of power between us. We drove back in silence, and I knew what would happen next. It always happened the same way.

Apologies would come through physical touch, making love to me like I was precious, whispering sweet promises in the dark about how things would change, how more time was needed. And I would accept it, because those moments of tenderness felt like the only love I'd ever known—conditional, secretive, always on someone else's terms.

Afterward, as the Unrequited Lover slept peacefully beside me, I lay awake staring at the ceiling, feeling more alone than I'd ever felt in my life. By morning, distance would return, phone checking anxiously, making sure no one had seen my car in the driveway.

This is what I call loving in shadows. Living in the spaces between daylight and darkness, existing only when convenient, being loved only when it costs nothing.

Last night, in a fit of rage that felt disturbingly familiar, I destroyed my apartment. Threw dishes, overturned furniture, cursed the day I ever met the Unrequited Lover. The isolation that followed was complete—sitting in the wreckage of my own making, realizing I had nowhere to run, no arms that would welcome me without conditions or secrets.

The Unrequited Lover had trained me well. I'd been taught that love was something you had to earn through silence, through accepting scraps, through never asking for too much. I'd learned that wanting to be claimed was "needy," that desiring public acknowledgment was "dramatic," that my pain was an inconvenience to be managed rather than a wound to be healed.

Just like Senior had taught me that love came with fists and threats and basement chains.

Just like Mama had taught me that love meant accepting the unacceptable to keep peace.

The Unrequited Lover was my drug of choice—the familiar poison that tasted like all the love I'd ever known.

I woke this morning with dread in my heart, knowing I'd have to face Dr. Reed and tell her about the date, knowing she'd somehow connect it to my past. The skeletons in my closet were clawing at the door, their screaming anguish no longer deafening but demanding to be heard.

"How did your date go, Mario?" Dr. Reed asks gently as I settle into my usual spot on her couch.

The question hangs in the air like smoke. I tell her about the entanglement, about the months of stolen moments and midnight confessions, about falling so deeply in love with the Unrequited Lover only to be met with shame and secrecy. About the restaurant scene, about my desperate plea for acknowledgment, about having my pain dismissed as "being dramatic."

"The Unrequited Lover said what we have is special because it's private," I tell Dr. Reed, my voice hollow. "I was called needy for wanting validation from other people. But it's not about other people—it's about not being someone's dirty little secret. It's about being worthy of being claimed. It's what I call loving in shadows."

Dr. Reed nods thoughtfully. "Tell me more about how this relationship makes you feel."

"Like I'm back in that basement," I whisper. "Hidden away, only valuable when needed for something, silenced when I ask for too much. The Unrequited Lover loves me in the dark and pretends I don't exist in the light. Just like..." I trail off, the connection hitting me like a physical blow.

"Just like your family did," she finishes gently.

"This particular type of attachment pattern is typically associated with not being loved properly as a child," she says, adjusting her glasses. "How do you view your relationship with your mother?"

The question hits like a punch to the gut. "I never truly understood why Mama didn't leave Senior," I say, my voice barely above a whisper. "I have ideas about why she couldn't permanently protect me from his abuse, but..." I trail off, the familiar confusion and anger rising.

"Tell me about one of those times, Mario. When did you first realize she was trapped too?"

I close my eyes, letting my mind wander back to a memory I've buried deep.

Memory: The Book Incident

I was six years old when I threw a book at my teacher at Garfield Elementary.

I'd gotten a "B" on my assignment. In our house, anything less than an "A" for me meant a beating. I knew what was waiting for me at home—Senior 's belt, Senior 's fists, Senior 's rage about how I was "too stupid" and "would never amount to nothing." The "B" on my paper felt like a death sentence.

So when Mrs. Henderson started talking about happy families, about fathers who come home and read bedtime stories, something inside me snapped. Here she was, painting pictures of loving fathers while

I sat there knowing mine would probably put me in the hospital for bringing home that "B."

The book left my hand before I could stop it, sailing across the classroom and slamming into the blackboard with a loud crack.

It wasn't premeditated—just pure rage exploding from my small body like lava from a volcano. All I could think was: *How dare you talk about loving fathers when mine is a monster? How dare you make me pretend that's normal when my normal is terror?*

The principal's paddle was nothing compared to what I knew was waiting for me at home. As each strike landed across my bottom, all I could think about was Senior 's hands, Senior 's belt, Senior 's fists. This was just the warm-up act.

When Mama picked me up, the anger and frustration were written all over her face. The duality of her roles—loving mother and dutiful wife—was a burden too heavy for her small shoulders to carry. She gripped the steering wheel of our gray four-door sedan with tinted windows, her knuckles white, her jaw clenched.

"Mario, what were you thinking?" she asked, but her voice was tired, defeated. "You know what this means when we get home. You know what happens when you act out at school."

I knew. Senior was home, working on the car in the garage. I brushed past him as we pulled in, rushing to my room, hoping against hope that maybe this time would be different. Maybe the "B" plus the school incident wouldn't equal the catastrophe I knew was coming.

Of course, Junior went to the garage to inform Senior that I'd gotten in trouble at school. I sat on my bed, listening to their voices drift through the walls—Senior 's anger, Mama's attempts at explanation, her agreement that punishment was necessary.

The walls closed like a prison. The silence was deafening. Then, in a moment of pure terror, the door burst open.

My heart almost left my body, my lungs deflated of air, and I looked up to see the monster standing there. He stormed in, rebuked me with words that cut like knives, and then surprisingly handed Mama the belt.

For a brief moment, elation rose in my chest. The whooping was coming from Mama, not him. The severity wouldn't be as bad.

Within five strokes, the door burst open again.

Like a seasoned demon with many tools in his repertoire, Senior entered the room with a rubber hose from the car he'd been working on. "Drop your pants," he ordered.

My heart dropped. *Could this be real?*

Mama stood there in shock, tears flowing down her face, begging him not to use the rubber hose. But he ordered her out of the room, and within the confines of those four walls, trust and familial ties were shattered forever. The line between father and son was obliterated.

What happened next broke me in ways that six years of life hadn't prepared me for: torture, methodical and merciless. The rubber hose cut through the air with a whistle before each impact, leaving welts that swelled immediately, angry and purple, some splitting open and bleeding down my small legs.

With every strike across my back, butt, and legs, I felt pieces of my soul dying. I clenched the sheets so hard my knuckles turned white, screaming until my voice gave out, then screaming silently as my body convulsed with each blow.

"I'm so sick of you," he snarled between strikes, his voice devoid of any human warmth. "You're gonna get it right or die trying."

I wanted to die. In that moment, death felt like mercy. I lay there praying—not only to God, but to anyone, anything that might hear the desperate pleas of a broken child. *Someone come save me. Someone make this stop. Someone see what's happening to me.*

But no one came.

The realization was birthed in that room: **no one will save me**. This truth would carry with me through every day of my life, shaping every relationship, every moment of vulnerability, every plea for help that would die in my throat before it could escape.

I heard my mother's voice like a lifeline, pleading for him to stop. Through my tears, I saw my brother standing in the hallway, eating a popsicle—Senior 's favorite treat. What happened next still haunts me.

In what was perceived as sheer defiance—Mama trying to end my torment—Senior found a new target. In one swift move, he changed to repeatedly punching and dragging her across the carpet into their room, where he continued to enact his retribution.

I sat frozen on the bed. When I finally got up and looked back at where I'd been sitting, I saw bloodstains on the sheets, letting me know I was seriously wounded.

Through the screaming and yelling from the adjacent room, Junior grabbed me and took me to the bathroom, helping me clean my wounds that stretched across my back all the way down to my legs. The swollen, hurtful, and bleeding bruising was evidence of what I'd endured, proof of what my body had survived.

He gave me a half-hearted smile of pity.

I cried harder, knowing that my attempt to be saved had only made things worse for Mama.

In that moment, a barrier was created in me that would last for decades. A wall built from guilt and terror whispered: *Never be open about your feelings. Never bring someone else in. Through you and because of you, they will be hurt. Your dear mother is being punished because you dared to hope for rescue.*

This was the day I learned that seeking help was dangerous—not only for me, but for anyone who tried to love me.

For a moment, I heard no screaming, and that concerned me more than the violence had.

I rushed to their room and was met by Senior in the hallway. He ordered us not to enter the room. I watched him go to the bathroom and change his blood-soaked shirt, wash his hands. The clear water that poured from the faucet into the white basin turned red like the rivers of Egypt when he put his hands underneath.

He didn't acknowledge me, gave Michael a hug, and left.

I watched out the window for him to leave, then rushed to their room. Michael attempted to stop me, regurgitating his father's order, but I yelled that I didn't care and shoved him out of the way.

I opened the door with trembling fear.

The bedroom was huge, very reminiscent of the '80s: king-sized bed, box TV, retro curtains. I climbed up to my mother.

Adults tell children about monsters—scary creatures alien to our eyes. But I learned that monsters walk among us and sometimes take the form of someone who's supposed to love us.

Her face was bruised and swollen beyond recognition. She lay there holding her ribs, shivering. She looked at me out of her good eye, blood still running from her mouth, and told me I wasn't supposed to be there. She ordered me out of the room and not to return.

"Listen to your father, Mario," she whispered through swollen lips. "I'm not gonna be well for a couple of days. Keep him happy, and you'll have nothing to worry about."

She told me she loved me.

There was a sound outside, and fear streaked across her face. She sat up slightly and said, "Hurry, get out of here. He's back."

I ran like a slave toward freedom and watched as he entered the room with a 40 oz bottle of Mickey's beer—the green bottle that was Mama's favorite. Then came music, slow music, the kind old folks liked.

I heard tapping on the wall, and Michael said something I didn't understand then but would comprehend later: "Eww, they're doing it."

I didn't know what that meant. All I knew was that somehow, impossibly, Mama forgave him. Again.

"Mario, this concept you've named—'loving in shadows'—it perfectly captures the toxic dynamic you've been trapped in," Dr. Reed says, leaning forward with intensity. "You've been existing only in the spaces between light and darkness, being loved only when it's convenient and costs nothing."

She pauses, letting the words sink in like seeds in fertile soil.

"The dynamics between abuser and abused are complex, Mario. Sex can be weaponized as part of the cycle of abuse. Love becomes confused with pain, intimacy with survival."

I nod with questionable enthusiasm, my body language shifting in ways I hope she doesn't notice. But Dr. Reed has been doing this too long. She catches the way I avert my eyes, the way my shoulders tense, the way my hands clench involuntarily.

She adjusts her glasses and makes a note in her pad. "We'll talk about this more in the future. There are layers here we need to explore."

That topic is one I did not want to talk about. I wish she hadn't noticed. Sexual abuse was part of my story, and I didn't want to talk about it. Not now. Not *ever*.

"This is going to be a recurring theme in your healing journey, Mario. You've learned to accept shadow love because it's all you've ever known. But God didn't create you to hide in the shadows. The Scripture says, 'Let your light so shine before men.' You were meant to be loved in the full light of day, openly, proudly, without shame."

I feel a fissure crack open in the wall I've built around my heart, but also terror at what might spill out if that wall completely crumbles.

"The Unrequited Lover, your father, even the family dynamics that kept your mother trapped taught you that love belongs in the shadows. But real love? Real love steps into the light. Real love claims you publicly. Real love doesn't make you beg for acknowledgement."

She adjusts her glasses again, her voice taking on the cadence of prophecy. "Your journey is about learning to step out of those shadows and demand the love you deserve. No more accepting crumbs. No more being grateful for conditional affection. It's time to walk into the light, Mario."

But I know there are darker shadows she hasn't discovered yet. Shadows I've buried so deep I sometimes convince myself they never existed at all.

"Do you see the connection between your confusion of abuse with love, and your current situation with the Unrequited Lover?" she asks.

The question breaks something else inside me. I see the pattern now. The way I chase people who can't or won't love me openly. The way I equate secrecy with intimacy, conditional affection with what I deserve. The Unrequited Lover not only rejected me last night—the very idea that I was worthy of being chosen publicly, proudly, was rejected.

"I've been trained," I whisper, the realization hitting like a sledgehammer. "Just like Senior trained Mama. I've been taught that love is something you have to earn through silence, through accepting scraps, through never asking for too much. I was made grateful for whatever crumbs of affection got thrown my way."

I think about all those nights I lay awake beside the Unrequited Lover, feeling more alone than I'd ever felt, watching peaceful sleep while I agonized over why I wasn't enough. Like I used to lie awake as a child, wondering what I'd done wrong, why I wasn't worthy of protection, why love always came with conditions and threats.

"The Unrequited Lover is my drug of choice," I continue, the words pouring out now. "The familiar poison that tastes like all the love I've ever known. Conditional. Secretive. Always on someone else's terms. Always loving in shadows."

I break down crying, and in a breach of professional decorum, Dr. Reed embraces me.

I needed that.

"Your mother loved you, Mario," she whispers. "But she was trapped in a system that gave her no good choices. Leaving meant poverty, homelessness, losing her children to a man who had all the power. Staying meant watching her babies suffer. She chose what she thought was survival for all of you."

"But why didn't anyone help her?" I sob into her shoulder. "Why didn't anyone help us?"

"Because the world wasn't ready to see what was happening behind closed doors. Because women like your mother were taught that keeping the family together was more important than their own safety. Because the very people who should have protected you—the church, the community, the family—were part of the system that kept her trapped."

I pull back, looking at her through tear-blurred eyes. "So what now? How do I stop choosing people who can't love me the way I need to be loved?"

"We start by understanding that the conditional, violent, secretive love you experienced as a child isn't real love at all. Real love doesn't hurt or require you to hide. Real love doesn't make you beg for basic respect and acknowledgment."

She hands me a tissue. "And Mario? That little boy who tried to save his mama by getting between her and her abuser? That boy's instincts were right. Love should protect, not harm. You need to learn what healthy love looks like."

For the first time in my adult life, I began to understand that maybe I'm worthy of a love that doesn't come with conditions, secrecy, or pain. Maybe I deserve a love that chooses me openly, proudly, completely. Maybe that little boy in the bloodstained bedroom deserved better than he got. Maybe the man sitting in this office deserves better too.

Chapter 3: The Whole Circus

Old habits are hard to break.

I spent the last two weeks trying to get ahold of the Unrequited Lover. Even though I told Dr. Reed I would end this relationship, sometimes you get an itch that just needs to be scratched. There was something about this person that made me feel so complete. I've been driving myself crazy wondering where they are, what they're doing, and why they're not contacting me.

When one of my friends called and invited me out to dinner for a celebration for one of our coworkers, I was bored and said sure.

I arrived at the restaurant and, to my surprise, the Unrequited Lover was there. My heart was elated. And admittedly, my primal desires were equally elated. But confusion surfaced because I couldn't understand why I never got any return phone calls.

We sat through dinner, and throughout all my efforts, I never got any acknowledgement from my eye gazes. I really wanted to cause a scene because if you're going to act like a clown, I'm going to be the whole circus. The Unrequited Lover knows this about me, so why are they trying me in public? I don't know, but I will be Bozo the Clown if I have to be.

I ordered a couple of drinks, and with each Long Island Iced Tea, the more bold and pissed I became. The Unrequited Lover left to go to the bar, and this was my opportunity to check this situation. I watched them walk away, their confident stride making my blood boil even more. *After weeks of silence, they had the audacity to sit at the same table and act like I was invisible?* Not today.

I followed them to the bar, the alcohol giving me liquid courage and a dangerous sense of invincibility. The bartender was busy with other customers, giving us a moment of relative privacy in the crowded space.

"Bitch," I approached and said, stepping close enough that they had to acknowledge my presence, "long time no see. I hope you got insurance on your phone 'cause clearly it's broken because you haven't returned my phone calls."

The Unrequited Lover's body language shifted immediately—shoulders tensing, eyes darting around to see who might be watching. This was their worst nightmare: their secret being exposed in public, their carefully constructed image being threatened.

"Mario, please," they whispered urgently, *"not here. Not now."*

"Oh, *now* you know my name?" I laughed bitterly. "Funny how you remember it when you're scared of being embarrassed."

With the ease of someone totally unbothered, they tried to turn away, but a look of detached disgust crossed their face as if I was some mere peasant beneath their attention. That look—that dismissive, condescending look—was the match that lit the dynamite.

"Don't you dare turn your back on me," I said, my voice rising enough to make them nervous. "You don't get to ghost me for two weeks and then act like I don't exist."

"You're drunk," they said, trying to sound calm but I could hear the panic creeping in. "You're making a scene."

"I'm making a scene?" I stepped closer, invading their personal space. "Baby, you haven't seen a scene yet. Because regardless of whatever I've been through, I was never someone you could forget. And if I have to cause a scene in public to get your attention, trust and believe I will."

The bartender glanced our way, sensing the tension. Other patrons were starting to notice. This was exactly what the Unrequited Lover feared most—public exposure, their reputation being questioned, people asking uncomfortable questions about who I was and why I was so upset.

I grabbed the Unrequited Lover's arm, not hard enough to hurt but firm enough to make my point. "So we gonna do this?" My face was filled with the promise of following through with a performative act here at Applebee's. "You gonna keep pretending you don't know me, or are we gonna address this like adults?"

I met their unbotheredness with a challenging look, much like two lions facing off in the jungle. The tension was thick enough to cut with a knife. Someone was going to give in, or someone was about to get mauled.

The Unrequited Lover's eyes darted around the bar again, calculating the risk. They could see I was serious, could see that the alcohol had stripped away my usual filter and willingness to be dismissed.

"Okay, okay," they finally whispered, sensing that I was not the one to play with at this moment. They acquiesced and begged me not to cause a scene, to go ahead and leave, promising to call me later.

"Call me later?" I laughed loud enough to turn a few heads. "That's what you said last time. And the time before that. Your 'later' never comes, does it?"

"Mario, please—"

"Please what? Please continue to be your dirty little secret? Please continue to accept your crumbs while you live your real life with other people?"

They were visibly sweating now, their carefully controlled façade cracking under the pressure.

Typically, I would acquiesce as the weaker person in this relationship. I've learned over time that the person who cares the least typically holds the most amount of power. But tonight, I had several drinks, I didn't drive, and they had already pissed me off. So, I wasn't going anywhere.

"You know what?" I said, stepping back and raising my voice a little more. "Don't worry about calling me later. Don't worry about explaining. Don't worry about anything. Just know that this—I gestured between us—this little game you play? It's over."

I grabbed my refill from the bar and walked back to the table, leaving them standing there, shaken and exposed in a way they'd never been before.

The power dynamic had shifted, if only for a moment. And it felt damn good.

At the table, the Unrequited Lover started getting real jittery, and I couldn't quite put my finger on it, but something was off. Then one of our coworkers, Sherry, got up to give a toast.

The toast was for the Unrequited Lover.

I didn't know what was going on. We hadn't talked in weeks. Last I heard, they were up for a promotion, so I thought this was a dinner celebrating their promotion. I got up, ready to toast my secret boo's promotion.

The words that left Sherry's mouth totally crushed my soul.

Sherry toasted congratulations to the Unrequited Lover on their *engagement*.

At this moment, I did not know God, but I felt God, Jesus, the Holy Spirit, and all twelve of the disciples hold me back from flipping that table over and cussing everybody at Applebee's out. Because I knew that my secret lover did not get engaged after ghosting me for two weeks and then publicly acknowledging their lover as their fiancé, after keeping me in the shadows for several years. I was beyond hurt, frustrated, and fearful for the Unrequited Lover's life had I found them in the parking lot when I left Applebee's.

I rode back home at 10:00 PM and immediately got on the phone and left a voicemail message for Dr. Reed, advising that I needed an immediate meeting first thing in the morning. Typically, I dreaded these meetings, but I really needed a session.

I finished off a bottle and a half of Mad Dog 20/20 and smoked a Black & Mild to calm my nerves. Sitting in my apartment, I reminisced about all the good times—well, what I envisioned as good times—I had with this person. To be done in this manner was the absolute ultimate betrayal.

I turned my phone off because I didn't want to hear from anyone, especially the Unrequited Lover, who I knew was going to blow up my phone trying to explain.

Morning came, and as the sun trespassed through the curtains in my apartment, shrouding my face and kissing my cheeks, I arose, peering out my window and wondering what life was going to bring me today. I glanced down at my phone and smirked, knowing that I would probably have several messages, all trying to sway the Unrequited Lover's actions and explain away the events of last night.

The phone powered up and immediately showed two missed calls and one text message. *You know better*, I thought. *You got some explaining to do.*

I listened to my voicemail messages. The first one was my mama calling me about some drama in the family, which I didn't care about. *Delete.*

The second one was my friend Toni wanting to talk about the Unrequited Lover's engagement, which I didn't want to talk to anybody about because I didn't want to acknowledge it. Acknowledging it would give it life, and I wanted it to die just like I wanted the fiancé to die. *Delete.*

Now on to the text message, which I knew was from the Unrequited Lover.

But the message was a text reminder to come to Dr. Reed's office at 10 AM.

I almost threw my phone against the wall. I knew the Unrequited Lover did not ignore this situation and not even have the *decency* to address it with me.

So I did what any crazed lover would do—I called the Unrequited Lover.

My phone call went immediately to voicemail. I tried for the next couple of hours, and each call went directly to voicemail, which led me to believe I was blocked.

You've got to be kidding me. You do this to me and you block me?

I pulled up to Dr. Reed's office, and for an up-and-coming urban practitioner, her office was a testament to both success and intention. The building itself was a sleek, three-story structure with floor-to-ceiling windows that seemed to invite light into every corner—a stark contrast to the shadows I'd been living in.

Walking through the glass doors, I was greeted by a reception area that whispered elegance without shouting ostentation. The furniture was modern but warm—rich mahogany wood paired with soft leather chairs in deep burgundy. Abstract art pieces adorned the walls, each one seeming to tell a story of struggle transformed into beauty. A large piece behind the reception desk caught my eye: swirls of dark blues and blacks giving way to brilliant golds and whites, like a storm breaking into dawn.

The lighting was soft but purposeful, casting no harsh shadows, and I noticed how every corner of the space felt illuminated. Fresh orchids sat on the reception desk, their white blooms pristine and hopeful. The entire space smelled of lavender and something I couldn't quite place—maybe sandalwood—creating an atmosphere that was both professional and almost sacred.

Dr. Reed's personal office continued the theme. Her mahogany desk was substantial but not imposing, adorned with a simple cross, a framed Scripture verse that read, "Weeping may endure for a night, but joy comes in the morning," and a small plant that somehow thrived despite being indoors. Behind her chair hung her degrees—a Ph.D. in Clinical Psychology from Howard University, a Master's in Divinity from Duke, various certifications that spoke to her commitment to both mind and spirit.

The couch where I typically sat was positioned to catch natural light from the window, and I realized this wasn't accidental. Everything in this space was designed to draw people out of darkness and into light.

I walked into the office, and Dr. Reed immediately jumped into professional mode and asked me what was going on and what was the urgency.

I explained to her all the events from last night. I left no detail unturned. I felt if she was going to help me, she needed all the details, and I'm not one to shy away from any of my questionable behavior. She toggled between nods, uh-huhs, and looks of disapproval.

After I was done, I sat back nonchalantly.

Dr. Reed finished taking notes and sat back. "So what brings you here today?"

I didn't understand her question. I had explained to her exactly what happened.

Sitting back unbothered, she looked me in my eyes and said, "I provided you the tools to not go down this dark road at all. At our last meeting, I advised and you agreed that you would not be in contact with the Unrequited Lover. You've ignored my suggestion. You have not put into practice any of the techniques that I provided to you."

She leaned forward, her voice taking on the tone of someone who had reached the end of her patience.

"I get paid regardless of whether you implement any of my suggestions. I encourage you to get the most out of these sessions and not waste your money. I could sit here and tell you what you did wrong and advise you on how not to do this again, but you already know this. We've been down this road before."

The silence hung between us like a challenge.

"So my question to you today is: What can I tell you now that I have not already told you? What tools can I provide you that you will not use the next time this comes up? I have patients who really do need me, and I made time for you today when it wasn't necessary."

Her words hit like physical blows, each one landing with precision.

"At what point are you going to fight back at life and not fall back down the road of the snares that have plagued your whole life?"

I was dumbfounded, offended, and upset. But the truth of her words could not be denied.

I apologized, and with grace and manner, she retorted that it was not necessary. She wanted me to be better and healed, and she was here for me throughout the process. But I must take the process seriously and implement all the appropriate tools.

She advised once again not to contact the Unrequited Lover. "How are things at work going to be with this new dynamic, since you both work together?"

That was something I had not thought about. I wasn't sure I was mature enough to let this slide at work.

It seemed like I kept messing things up in life—my poor decisions, my anger, and now the drinking, which was something from my past that I didn't want to be a struggle point for me. Alcoholism had been an issue with my mother. Through the abuse and torment that we experienced for ten to twelve years of my adolescent life, it had forged a dependency on alcohol for her. One which I did not want to carry.

Dr. Reed provided some insights on the vices of using alcohol to numb the pain and equated that back to episodes in which my mother would be drunk or passed out to escape the reality of what was going on in our household.

"Mario, you're repeating patterns," she said gently. "Your mother used alcohol to escape Senior 's abuse. You're using alcohol to escape the pain of loving someone who can't love you properly. Do you see the connection?"

The truth hit me like cold water.

"The Unrequited Lover may be engaged to someone else, but you're still chained to them emotionally. You're still living in that basement, Mario, just with different walls."

She leaned forward, her voice taking on the cadence of someone who understood both psychology and spiritual warfare.

"Let me share something with you from a spiritual perspective, Mario. The Bible tells us in Proverbs that 'as a man thinks in his heart, so is he.' You've been thinking like a victim for so long that you've become addicted to victimhood. You're addicted to the familiar pain because it's easier than the unfamiliar work of healing."

She reached for her Bible on the desk, her fingers finding the passage with practiced ease.

"First Corinthians tells us that 'God will not allow you to be tempted beyond what you can bear, but with every temptation, He will provide a way of escape.' Mario, last night at that restaurant was your temptation. The way to escape was walking away when you saw them. But you chose the familiar pattern instead."

Her words cut deep, but there was compassion in her delivery.

"You've been operating in what I call 'trauma loyalty'—being faithful to the very thing that's destroying you. You're loyal to patterns that don't serve you because they're familiar. You're loyal to people who hurt you because you mistake intensity for intimacy."

She set the Bible down and looked directly into my eyes.

"The enemy of your soul wants you to believe that you're only worthy of shadow love, that you should be grateful for crumbs. But God says you're fearfully and wonderfully made. God says you're the head and not the tail. God says no weapon formed against you shall prosper."

I felt something stirring in my chest—part conviction, part hope.

"Mario, what happened last night wasn't about the Unrequited Lover getting engaged. It was about you getting a front-row seat to see what happens when someone chooses to love in the light instead of the shadows. They chose someone they could be proud of publicly. The question is: when will you choose someone—starting with yourself—that you can be proud of?"

She paused, letting the weight of her words settle.

"This situation is painful, but it's also purposeful. Sometimes God has to close doors we keep trying to force open. Sometimes He has to remove people from our lives who are blocking our blessings. The Unrequited Lover wasn't just unavailable emotionally—they were a spiritual roadblock to your destiny."

Dr. Reed stood and walked to her window, gazing out at the natural light streaming in.

"Your assignment, Mario, is to stop trying to resurrect what God has already buried. Stop trying to revive relationships that He's already pronounced dead. Your healing is waiting on the other side of your obedience to let go."

I left Dr. Reed's office and immediately tried one more time to call the Unrequited Lover. It went straight to voicemail. I deleted the number and took that small victory as a step in the right direction.

But as I sat in my car in her parking lot, her words began to sink deeper than my initial resistance had allowed. *Trauma loyalty.* The phrase echoed in my mind like a bell that wouldn't stop ringing. Had I been faithful to the very thing that was destroying me?

I thought about all the nights I'd laid awake, making excuses for the Unrequited Lover's behavior. All the times I'd convinced myself that their inability to love me publicly was somehow romantic, somehow special. All the ways I'd twisted their rejection into evidence of a deeper connection that others couldn't understand.

You're addicted to victimhood because it's easier than the unfamiliar work of healing.

The truth of that statement felt like surgery without anesthesia. I had been addicted—to the drama, to the uncertainty, to the familiar pain that felt more like home than actual peace ever could. I'd been choosing the devil I knew over the God I was afraid to trust.

Sitting there in the car, I began to understand what Dr. Reed meant about spiritual roadblocks. The Unrequited Lover hadn't just been emotionally unavailable—they had been a distraction from my purpose, a detour from my destiny. Every moment I spent chasing someone who ran from me was a moment I wasn't spending becoming who God created me to be.

I thought about the way I'd felt at that restaurant, the desperation in my voice when I confronted them at the bar. That wasn't love—that was desperation masquerading as devotion. That was trauma dressed up as romance.

Sometimes God has to close doors we keep trying to force open.

Maybe the blocked phone number wasn't rejection—maybe it was protection. Maybe the engagement wasn't abandonment—maybe it was liberation. Maybe God had been trying to free me from a prison I didn't even realize I was in.

It was at this moment that I started to evaluate and understand what my true worth was. It cannot be tied to a person, an object, an experience, or any other type of temporal element. Who I am and what I must become and my worth are tied to who I see myself as. Only I can determine what my true worth is. Its dependency is not based on anyone else but myself.

But more than that—my worth was tied to how God saw me. Dr. Reed had said I was fearfully and wonderfully made, that I was the head and not the tail. If God thought I was worthy of love that didn't hide in shadows, then who was I to settle for less?

I have to shake this off. But the feeling of rejection invites my long-term friend loneliness back in. And loneliness breeds suffering. And suffering invites depression. And we all sit at the table called isolation and welcome in the atmosphere of despair.

I could feel them gathering—these familiar spirits that had kept me company for so long. Rejection, loneliness, suffering, depression, isolation, despair. They were like old friends knocking at my door, comfortable and known.

But Dr. Reed's words cut through their whispers: Stop trying to resurrect what God has already buried.

These feelings, these patterns, these addictions to familiar pain—God had already pronounced them dead. My job wasn't to keep visiting their graves or trying to bring them back to life. My job was to walk away from the cemetery and into the light.

But I cannot exist here. I need to move forward. This was unfortunate but needed. And I have to reframe the situation in my mind so that I can see this differently—as a way for me to rebuild myself.

This wasn't about reframing my thoughts—this was about spiritual warfare. This was about choosing to believe God's voice over the enemy's lies. This was about walking in faith instead of familiar dysfunction.

The Unrequited Lover chose to love someone else in the light while keeping me in the shadows. They chose their reputation over my heart. They chose their comfort over my dignity.

Maybe they did me a favor by freeing me from a spiritual prison I'd been too blind to see.

Maybe being blocked from their phone means I can finally block them from my heart.

Maybe their engagement to someone else means I can finally become engaged with my own healing, my own purpose, my own destiny.

Maybe their choice to love in the light with someone else means I can finally stop accepting love that only exists in the shadows.

Dr. Reed was right—I have been living in that basement, just with different walls. But basements have exits. Shadows have sources of light. And every prison has a key—sometimes we have to stop being so loyal to our chains that we refuse to use it.

And circus acts? Well, they're performances.

It's time to stop performing for an audience that will never applaud.

It's time to step off the stage and into my own life, into God's plan for my life.

The show is over. The circus is leaving town.

And I'm not going with it.

I'm staying here, in the light, learning to love myself the way God loves me—openly, proudly, without shame.

The circus is leaving town, and I'm not going with it. I'm staying here, in the light, learning to love myself the way God loves me—openly, proudly, without shame. The Unrequited Lover taught me to perform for love, to be grateful for whatever attention I could get. But I'm done being the entertainment in someone else's show. It's time to write my own story.

Chapter 4: Walking on Broken Glass

This morning feels different. For the first time in months, I wake up with something that feels foreign to me—hope. Dr. Reed's session yesterday left me feeling like I actually have tools to fight with instead of just surviving.

I decided to take a walk at For-Mar Nature Preserve before heading to work. I need to ground myself in something real, something peaceful, before I face what I know will be a test of everything Dr. Reed taught me.

The morning air is crisp, and I watch as two kids play together on the trail ahead of me—laughing, chasing each other, completely carefree. For a moment, it takes me back to an imaginary time when Junior and I might have had this kind of relationship. But then reality sets in. This is not who we are. We never were those kinds of brothers.

Thoughts and feelings of dread, worry, and despair begin to creep up and ruin the almost ethereal feeling I'm having right now. I have to go to work today, and I have resolved in my head that regardless of what happened the other night regarding the Unrequited Lover, I am not going to allow this scene to taint my work environment.

Pulling into the parking lot, I sit in my car and contemplate how I'm going to make it through today. Several coworkers walk by and give me casual waves, and in likewise fake fashion, I wave back. Truth be told,

I don't really like anyone here. I only came here for work. Most of the people here are catty and gossipy, and I don't want any part of it.

Here I resolve in my mind: I'm going to walk into work and own it. I'm not going to let anyone take me off my square. All of these Scriptures and powerful words that Dr. Reed provided me give me courage and resolve to go into work with the right spirit and mind.

I take a deep breath, grab my bookbag, and stride toward the building like I own it. Every step is intentional, my back straight, my head high. I am not a victim today. I am a winner walking into battle armed with God's truth and Dr. Reed's wisdom.

The automatic doors slide open, and I step into the lobby with the confidence of a man who knows his worth. I nod at security, acknowledge colleagues with professional courtesy, and head toward my cubicle like a king returning to his throne.

But as I approach my workspace, I am almost stopped dead in my tracks when I see the Unrequited Lover standing there in full display. I overhear the conversation concerning the joy they feel regarding their engagement.

This entire scene is contrived. There is no reason for this little meeting right outside my office. The purpose has to be nefarious because there is no reason to be near my workspace to discuss these pending nuptials. The Unrequited Lover has their own office on a different floor.

I am not going to allow you to pull me into a place that I am fighting to not go back to.

I brush past the group with a nod of acknowledgment toward them, my stride never breaking, my composure intact.

"Well, good morning," the Unrequited Lover extends to me.

The unmitigated gall for you to speak to me.

It is beyond my belief and understanding—the brazen boldness of this person to act as if there are no underlying issues. The sense of security that the Unrequited Lover has in the workplace is mind-boggling. And true to form, although I would normally respond in kind, the level of decorum at work is a level that I will not breach. And the Unrequited Lover knows this.

I provide a dry, "Good morning" and quickly enter my office, rolling my belongings onto the desk and falling into my chair. A deep sigh attempts to assuage the anger that is building up inside me. I begin to mumble and talk to myself, reciting some of the Scriptures Dr. Reed shared with me.

A gentle knock on the door interrupts this, and I turn around in my chair. Standing right there, this close, is the Unrequited Lover.

What the hell are you doing?

I respond, "How can I help you?"

The Unrequited Lover has a smirk on their face and responds, "You can meet me in my office in the next five minutes. We need to have a meeting."

Perhaps a meeting between your lips and my ass. But before I can respond, the Unrequited Lover leaves.

I sat there wondering what we could possibly talk about in your office. But a moment of human weakness begins to creep in as I remember intimate moments that we've experienced in this very office on the manager's floor. Unbridled, uninhibited passion was something we experienced numerous times. And in the back of my head, this feels like a buildup to one of those times. Every fiber of my being knows that if this is to go in that direction, I must resist. But the flesh is so weak.

Anger is displaced with anticipation and lust. My frowning face streaks with momentary delight as I walk down the hallway to the elevator to head to the third floor. It seems like it takes forever for the elevator to go from one to three. With each ding of the elevator, each moment, memories are playing of moments in which the Unrequited Lover and I had workday playtime. Just one more time.

The door opens. I exit and walk down the long hallway to the ostentatious office of the Unrequited Lover. The secretary, an older brown-hued woman, looks up. She's seen me numerous times. I'm not sure she knew what was going on in those offices, but she knew that I frequented them.

"I believe I have a meeting," I say.

She barely looks up and says, "They are waiting for you."

I say okay and keep it moving. But *they*? Who are *they*?

I walk into the office, and there sits the Unrequited Lover in the usual power position behind their otherwise unnecessarily large desk. And in the chair next to the desk is the VP of Human Resources.

My hope and dream of a romantic encounter shatters like glass on the floor.

"We need to have a conversation," says the Unrequited Lover.

I sit down and don't say a word.

"I wanted to have a meeting with you, and Sam is here for visibility purposes."

The words that follow hit me like physical blows:

"It has come to my attention that there have been various incidents concerning you and your behavior. I mentioned this to you before when you got into an argument with Marcus—I looked at that as a warning to you. And then we received numerous complaints last night regarding your behavior. You were belligerent, drunk, and inappropriate. I witnessed this myself. Based upon all of this information and the history, I regret to inform you that we have decided to let you go."

The room spins slightly as the words sink in.

"We would typically do an investigation, but the findings from multiple different sources seem to be credible, and it's not something we can tolerate any further. Last night was an official business function, and your behavior was not what we expect from our employees. It has been a pleasure having you with us, but security is in the hallway and they will walk you out. This termination is effective immediately. If you need anything or have any further questions, please reach out to human resources, who will be sending you a termination letter and package within the next three to five days."

The Unrequited Lover signals for security to come in.

I am at a total loss for words. They know the issue with Marcus was because Marcus found out about our supposed affair and tried to joke about it with me. When I corrected him, he got upset and got in my face, and the three of us got into an argument—not just me and Marcus. So this changing of the narrative is upsetting. And I truly doubt there were several complaints because the only person I was inappropriate with and the only person I was belligerent with was the Unrequited Lover.

This is payback.

If I were built differently, I would expose this entire illicit affair. I would tell HR about the numerous hookups in this office, the fudging of timecards that allowed me to sneak out, the late-night phone calls, the stolen kisses throughout the office. The Unrequited Lover was in a position of power over me and violated numerous rules that govern this organization. They should have been the one to be fired, not me. But my blind loyalty and who I am as a person will not allow me to expose our background and complicate not only my life but the Unrequited Lover's.

I rise up from the desk, and for a brief moment, both the Unrequited Lover and the VP are nervous because they think I'm going to perform.

I learned a long time ago not to give people what they expect. *You expect me to act a fool? You expect me to curse you out? You expect me to clear out my things and make accusations, all the while eventually claiming them as me being a disgruntled employee?* I will not give you the satisfaction of me showing my anger. I will not allow you to see me broken. I will not allow you to see me shed a tear. But what you will see is me walking out this door with my head held high. And I will pay you dust. No words shall be spoken.

I exit the room toward the elevator, past security. We get off on the first floor, and I walk toward my office. Security advises that I am not allowed to go into my office and that my personal belongings will be mailed to me.

"That's not going to happen," I retort. "My personal belongings will not be touched by anybody. I'm leaving here with what I came with, and no one is going to stop me. And if anybody puts their hands on me, we will have a problem. There are items that I don't want handled by anyone but myself. I'm grabbing them and leaving, and you can keep everything else."

The office becomes abuzz as I am escorted to my office and watched like a criminal as I pack up everything. My foes and detractors are watching, gossiping, and having such a good time.

The fiancé of the Unrequited Lover walks past my office. I take a pause to examine the differences between us. *Why were you chosen and I wasn't?* If looks could kill, we lock eyes for a moment, and a sheepish smile is extended to me. I return it. *It isn't your fault. The blame here rests on the Unrequited Lover. You probably didn't even know who I was.*

As I exit the office with my box and security carries another box, I wave at some of my coworkers that I enjoyed and say goodbye. I get in my car and drive off, knowing I will never return there.

The walls are beginning to close in, and this is another loss I have to take. But at this point, I have to rebuild. I reflect on what brought me to this point. How could I have been such a fool? I dissect the last two or three years of my life, inch by inch, moment by moment, kiss by kiss, looking for ways to discern what happened. What could I have done differently?

My phone rings, and I see Toni's name on the screen. She will be the only phone call that I would have taken. Anyone else would have been calling to get gossip. But Toni—Toni is different. She became my sister, the one who deeply cares about me when no one else seemed to notice I existed.

"Mario, what the hell happened? I heard they walked you out like some common criminal!" Her voice is fire and fury, ready to burn down the building for me.

I can't help but smile a little despite everything. This is exactly who Toni is—ride or die, no questions asked.

"It's complicated, Toni. But I'm okay—"

"No, you're not okay! And don't you dare try to protect them or make excuses. I've been watching that whole situation, and something stank about it from day one."

Within the two to three years we worked together, we transitioned from coworkers to family. But it was more than that—Toni became the big sister I never had, the protector I always needed but never found. She saw me in ways my own family never did.

I remember the day everything changed between us. I'd been having a particularly bad day—one of those days when the Unrequited Lover had been especially cold and dismissive. I was sitting in the break room, looking like I wanted to disappear, when Toni plopped down across from me.

"You know you don't have to take people's shit, right?" she said, not even looking up from her sandwich.

"What are you talking about?"

"I'm talking about how you let people walk all over you like you don't matter. Like you're not worthy of basic respect." She looked at me then, really looked at me. "But I see you, Mario. I see how smart you are, how kind you are, how much you care about doing good work. And if other people don't see that, that's their loss, not yours."

It was the first time in my adult life that someone had seen me—really seen me—and decided I was worth defending.

From that day forward, Toni became my fiercest advocate. She would check people who talked sideways about me. She celebrated my small victories like they were her own. When I got my first car, a white four-door LeSabre, I was so excited to show her because I knew she'd be genuinely happy for me.

"Give me the keys," she said immediately. "I want to test drive this because I want to make sure this is going to be a good car for you."

She took my keys before I could even approve and drove off in my car. I sat there dumbfounded like, "No, she didn't." But that's

Toni—she cares so hard it sometimes feels like an invasion, but it comes from a place of pure love.

She pulled back in ten minutes with a list. "Why is it idling so high? Take it back and ask them to make sure this is taken care of. And check the brake pads while you're at it. And Mario?" She looked at me seriously. "Don't let them talk you into buying any extra warranties you don't need. You call me if they try any funny business."

We both knew I wasn't gonna do half of what she told me, but Toni had to be Toni and protect her little brother in every way she could think of.

"I want to go and check the Unrequited Lover," she says now, her voice cutting through my memories. "This whole thing smells like retaliation."

Toni never knew about my romantic dealings with the Unrequited Lover. I kept those close to the vest, too ashamed to admit I was accepting crumbs from someone who couldn't even acknowledge me publicly. But she had her suspicions—Toni always had suspicions when something didn't feel right.

"Mario, I've been watching how that person treats you. Hot and cold, pulling you into meetings, then acting like you don't exist. That ain't normal supervisor behavior."

And like a true big sister, she was ready to go to war for her little brother, even without knowing the full story.

"Toni, you cannot do that. You have a family of your own that you have to take care of. I appreciate it, but—"

"Boy, don't you dare tell me what I can and cannot do when someone hurts my family. Because that's what you are, Mario. You're my family. And I protect my family."

The way she says it, so fierce and sure, makes my throat tight. When was the last time someone claimed me like that? When was the last time someone was willing to fight for me without expecting something in return?

"I'm gonna be okay, Toni."

"But no, this ain't gonna go down like this," she continues, and I can practically hear her wheels turning.

If I had a molecule of her strength and determination... Now, don't get me wrong, I am strong. But Toni's strength was different—it was enriched with boldness and confidence, things I'd never learned how to have. She wasn't afraid to take up space, to demand respect, to say "no" without apologizing for it.

I say she's my sister, but sometimes she felt more like my mentor, teaching me lessons about self-worth I never got at home. The way she moved through the world—unapologetic, protective, fierce—made me want to be braver.

"You know what your problem is, Mario?" she had told me once. "You think you have to earn love by being perfect, by never causing trouble, by making yourself small. But real love don't work like that. Real love sees your flaws and chooses you anyway. It sees your needs and meets them without you having to beg."

I think about that now as I sit in my car, jobless and feeling like my world is falling apart. Toni is proof that her own words are true—she saw all my brokenness and chose to love me anyway. She saw my needs and met them before I even knew I had them.

I want to turn around and drive to her house right now, let her wrap me in one of her fierce hugs and tell me everything's going to be okay. I need it at that moment—need to feel like someone's got my back. But I also know I need some alone time for reflection, need to sit with Dr. Reed's words and figure out how to rebuild from here.

"I love you, Toni," I tell her, and I mean it in ways she'll never fully understand.

"I love you too, little brother. And this ain't over. Mark my words."

I will say that I'm going to miss seeing her every day. But like she said—we're family. And family doesn't disappear just because your workplace does.

She taught me that love could be steady, consistent, unconditional. She taught me that I was worth protecting, worth celebrating, worth claiming publicly and proudly.

Maybe it's time I started believing her.

But even as I think that, the old familiar voice in my head starts whispering the truth I've been running from my whole life: *Everyone leaves me.*

The realization hits me like a physical blow, sitting here in my car outside Mama's house, listening to her party away her pain while I nurse mine in silence. It's no surprise that the Unrequited Lover left me for someone else. It's the pattern of my entire existence.

Junior left me. When we were kids, he chose Senior 's approval over protecting his little brother. When we got older, he chose his own life, his own family, his own path that didn't include looking back for the brother who needed him.

Mama left me. Not physically at first, but emotionally. She chose her bottles, her parties, her friends, her need to "live her life" over being present for the son who was still bleeding from wounds she couldn't heal because she was too busy nursing her own.

Senior left me. Abandoned the family when I was twelve, but the truth is he left me long before that—every time he chose violence over love, every time he looked at me with disgust instead of recognition, every time he treated me like I was something that didn't belong to him.

My family left me. Aunts, uncles, grandparents who saw what was happening and chose silence. Who knew a child was suffering and decided it wasn't their business. Who picked sides and I was never the side they picked.

There was a point in my life when I was essentially homeless. I was fourteen years old when Mama had to go to a shelter, but I was too old to go with her. So, I was passed around to "family"—relatives who made it clear they didn't want me in their homes. I was called names, told I was a burden, made to feel like an unwelcome guest in spaces that were supposed to offer refuge. I wasn't allowed to be at home in their homes, so I spent a lot of time walking aimlessly around Flint, carrying everything I owned in a backpack, wondering where I would sleep that night and whether anyone would ever want me to stay.

There was a point in my life where I was all I had in the world.

I spent a significant amount of time unprotected and alone. Learning that survival was a solo sport. Learning that counting on people was a luxury I couldn't afford. Learning that the only person who would never leave me was me—and even then, there were days I wanted to leave myself behind too.

This is the absolute truth, whether it's right or not, whether it's fair or not: EVERYONE LEAVES ME.

So why should the Unrequited Lover be any different? Why should I be surprised that someone else looked at me and decided I wasn't worth staying for? Why should I expect loyalty from someone who never even had the courage to claim me in the first place?

Maybe Dr. Reed is wrong. Maybe it's not about "loving in shadows." Maybe it's about the fact that I'm the kind of person people eventually walk away from. Maybe there's something fundamentally unlovable about me that I can't see but everyone else can.

Maybe the Unrequited Lover saw what everyone else sees—that I'm the temporary option, the placeholder, the person you're with until someone better comes along.

Sitting here, jobless and heartbroken, watching my mother choose Mickey's over me for the thousandth time, I realize that this is who I am: the person everyone leaves.

And the most devastating part? I keep being surprised by it. I keep hoping that this time will be different, that this person will stay, that I'll finally be worth choosing.

But I never am.

Even Toni, with all her fierce love and protection—she's still at that job, and I'm the one who got walked out. Even she couldn't save me from the pattern that's been following me my whole life.

Maybe loneliness isn't something that happens to me. Maybe loneliness is who I am.

Maybe everyone leaves me because that's exactly what I deserve.

I pull into Mama's house on the north side of Flint. I have to tell her what's going on. If she finds out some other way, there would be a problem.

As usual, Mama's got music blaring, liquor flowing, and her and her friends are outside in the front yard partying the day away. The scene hits me like a wall of chaos—it's barely noon on a Tuesday, and they're carrying on like it's New Year's Eve.

The boom box is perched on the front porch, pumping out Denise LaSalle at a volume that has the neighbors probably calling the police. Empty beer bottles and red Solo cups litter the small front yard. Mama's wearing a too-tight tank top and shorts that have seen better days, swaying to the music with a drink in her hand that's definitely not her first of the day.

Her crew is in full party mode: "Shorty," a woman who's about 4'10" but thinks she's 6 feet tall when she's drunk; "Phat Phat," whose nickname speaks for itself; Stephanie, who they call "Titty City" due to her almost double-FF cups on her size-10 build; and "White Karen," the one white woman in the group who somehow fits right in with this dysfunction.

They're dancing like they're at a concert they themselves headlined, completely oblivious to the fact that it's the middle of the day and most people are at work. The smell of cigarettes and liquor is offensive in the summer heat—it's almost 90 degrees, and with the alcohol, it's suffocating.

"Hey, Ma," I say, trying to get her attention over the music.

"Boy, what do you want?" she says, swaying dramatically to the music, her words already slurred.

"Mama, I need to talk to you," I responded.

"This is my jam," she says, continuing to sway rhythmically to the music with a drink in one hand.

"Mama, I really need to talk to you," I plead. But to no avail—the liquor and Denise win.

I move my chair under some shade and watch as her friends dance like they're performing for an invisible audience. Shorty is doing some sort of dance that might have been popular in 1985, while Phat Phat is trying to twerk but mostly just looks like she's having a seizure. Stephanie's dancing is hypnotic for all the wrong reasons, and White Karen is doing this weird thing with her arms that she probably thinks is sexy.

The longer I sit there, the more the scene depresses me. *Is this supposed to be the reality of where my life is at this point?* The once-vibrant woman that I remember told me years ago that it's time for her to live her life. And she fully embraced it, making sure that every moment of her life was a party.

But I wonder and want to remind her: *To what extent? Yes, you endured abuse, unimaginable strife with your husband. But at the same time, that was your husband—you selected him. You, as the adult, had the power to stay or leave. I, as a child, did not have a say in this. I did not pick my father. I could not leave when I wanted to. I needed the adults in the situation to be there for me.*

So yes, it's good that you are enjoying and living your life. But what life can I have when I was forced into adulthood at such a very young age? With my body broken, mental psyche shattered, and youthful innocence ripped away. I don't see much to have a party for.

As usual, I sit there and fade into the surroundings, always feeling nothing spectacular, blending into the nothingness of the shenanigans that are going on. There are times in my life when I used to wonder: *if I disappeared, would anybody miss me?*

Have you ever been so present and yet unseen at the same time? I was born into a family that neither side seemed to want me. On my father's side, he never claimed me as his son, treated me with such indifference—he really hated me. And I never understood why my brother basked in the overflow of love that he received from his father.

On my mother's side, I never fit in. I was always the taller one, thicker one, and quiet. It was as if I was planted into these families and nobody wanted me. Nobody understood where I fit—like a stray puzzle piece that didn't fit the picture on the box.

Junior was clearly everybody's favorite, and everybody tolerated me. It is difficult, even as an adult, to try to understand and rationalize this. So many people say that I need to move on. But how can I move on when I was raised and programmed to feel like I didn't matter? I was told as a child I was adopted and not wanted, which even today I question whether that's true or not.

I was treated subhuman. And in my darkest times when I needed help, no one was there. As I get older, I realize that existence is not enough. I need assurance. I need love. I need acceptance. I am a member of a family that I feel foreign in.

People mistake my standoffishness as being stuck up or prudish, when in actuality, I don't know how to fit in. I've never felt welcomed or wanted. I learned to live off momentary moments of kindness.

Sitting here watching Mama and her friends party away their pain, I realize we're not so different. She numbs her trauma with alcohol and loud music. I numbed mine with the Unrequited Lover's conditional affection.

We're both trying to survive the damage that Senior left behind.

But Dr. Reed's words echo in my mind: *Stop trying to resurrect what God has already buried.*

Maybe it's time to stop trying to get love from people who don't know how to give it.

Maybe it's time to stop settling for momentary moments of kindness and demand the consistent love I deserve.

Maybe it's time to leave this party too. But this time, I'm not running away from the pain—I'm walking toward something better. Something that doesn't require me to disappear into the background while everyone else celebrates their dysfunction. For the first time, leaving doesn't feel like abandonment—it feels like self-preservation.

Chapter 5: When Love Meant Blood

The walls of Dr. Reed's office feel like they're closing in. I've been avoiding this session for weeks, making excuses, canceling appointments, doing everything I can to stay away from the memories that are clawing at the door of my consciousness. But after losing my job, after the Unrequited Lover's betrayal, after sitting outside Mama's house realizing that everyone leaves me—I know I can't run anymore.

"Mario, we need to go deeper," Dr. Reed says gently, her voice cutting through my resistance." The surface wounds are healing, but there are infections underneath that we haven't touched yet."

I sink into the leather couch, feeling like a little boy again, small and powerless and afraid.

"I don't want to remember," I whisper.

"I know. But the memories are remembering you whether you want them to or not. They're controlling your life, your relationships, your sense of worth. It's time to take that power back."

She guides me through the meditation, her voice becoming distant as I sink deeper into the past, deeper into the darkness I've spent my whole life trying to escape.

It was a beautiful morning. The wind was blowing, it wasn't humid, and to a child, our backyard looked like an elaborate, expensive empire—multiple trees, cascades of long grass. Senior always kept animals and dogs in cages in the backyard. Outside of that scene, it was otherwise beautiful.

Me and Junior were running around playing when a voice echoed out the window: "Hey Mario, get in here and get some food and feed the dog Sheila."

I stopped playing and went to do as I was commanded. I got a big dish of food and took it over to Sheila. I unlocked the cage.

These were expensive cages, about six or seven feet tall, and in each cage in our backyard, a dog was chained inside. What most people didn't know was that Senior and his brother, who was a police officer, had routine dog fights in the garage of our house. His other police friends would come over late at night, and he would charge them for these fights. It was a big operation and party. These animals were used by Senior to participate in these dog fights, and he won lots of money from these particular fights.

I remember how he exercised his cruelty with these animals. Senior was quite handy with his hands—he constructed a treadmill in the basement that had an incline on it and attached above the treadmill was a spot to lock in the animals via chain around their necks. We would be responsible for bringing him an animal, and he would chain the animal to the treadmill. He would incline the treadmill to force the animal to run faster. If they didn't run faster, they would choke. He would take the rubber hose that he beat me with and start beating the animal to get them to run faster. The whole purpose of this was to strengthen them so that they could have more endurance during these particular fights.

Sheila was his prize possession. She would kill other dogs within a round or two. She was vicious.

As I walked into the cage, Sheila sat there looking at me as I put the dish down. Out of nowhere, she lunged toward me and bit me on my thigh. I fell back onto the fence, outside the reach of her chain, where she was gnawing to get at me.

I went into the house crying, to tell Senior that Sheila bit me.

The response I got was: "She only did that because you don't normally feed her. Why is it that Junior has to do all the work around this house? If you would see her normally like I tell you to, she would know you and she wouldn't attack you."

He left and went outside to go check on Sheila. As blood still ran down my leg, he returned with the rubber hose and immediately started beating me.

To this day, I still don't understand it, but I must surmise that it was because his dog got upset.

I went to the bathroom, still twitching and screaming from the deep lacerations of the rubber hose against my back and stomach. I almost forgot that I had a bite mark on my leg. When Mama came home and I told her what happened, she and Senior had World War III. She was at times fearful of him, but standing up for her children was something she always did, even if it meant she herself was going to get a beating. She argued with him ceaselessly throughout the day, and the end result was that she pushed him to get rid of Sheila since she presented a danger to the family now that she had tasted human blood.

I remember later that night, slightly inebriated with a glass in his hand, Senior said, "You little motherfucker, sleep tight, little nigga. I'm going to get you. You're fucking with my money," and closed the door.

The next morning, we rose to a normal day at the house. Tension, uncertainty, anger, and fear--these were the governing feelings of our house. It always felt like walking on eggshells. Mama announced that she was going to see her sister and said that she'd be taking us with her—meaning me and Junior. She reminded Senior that he needed to get rid of Sheila because she was still there.

With a slight smirk on his face, he said, "Sure, I'll get rid of her, but Junior's gonna stay with me. I need him. You can take Mario." He spoke with such sheer disdain and dismissiveness. Of course, Junior relished this alone time with his dear father and offered no objection. But any moment I could have away from Senior was one I was glad for.

We departed. I loved going on car trips with mama. We would see different sides of Flint, I liked listening to her blues music, and we got to see some of my cousins. Plus, it was a welcome distraction from being home with Junior, who really didn't want to play with me.

We arrived at my aunt's house on the north side of Flint during a family get-together. All my cousins were there, my aunts, my uncle, and my grandmother. And as usual, they asked where Junior was, which became the customary question amongst my mama's side of the family, as if I was a secondary sibling or the background singer in a duo.

As usual, the ladies went on the porch to sit and talk and have grown folks' conversation. I was running around playing with my cousins. As an added bonus, the crazy old man next door came and gave each one of us a food stamp and told us to go to the store and get ourselves some snacks. I couldn't wait to go home and tell Junior this! A food stamp, which was equivalent to a dollar in the '80s, seemed to mean we could buy up the whole store—a stark contrast to today's market.

When we got home and entered our house, there was a breezeway that connected the garage to the house and the basement, with several windows. Outside of those windows, I noticed that Sheila wasn't there.

"So did you get rid of that dog like I asked you to?" Mama asked as she entered the kitchen with Senior and Junior glued to some sporting event on TV.

He looked over and in a sarcastic tone said, "Your wish is my command."

Mama looked skeptical based upon her facial expression. I didn't care—I was happy that dog was gone. I wished all the others would leave too, but I must be transparent and true here: I didn't want all the dogs to leave. With them being there, it provided Senior a focus for his rage. When he was fighting dogs and training them, fewer beatings happened around the house. I surmised that he took his anger and aggression out on the animals, which left less for us in the house. It's disheartening for me to say that, but I was a little kid, and any reprieve I could get, I welcomed. Please don't judge me too hard.

Mama began to prepare dinner and looked over at me and said, "Go feed the cat and come help me in the kitchen."

As I went to grab the cat food, I noticed it was missing. I asked Junior where he put the cat food. Although Lucky was mine and my mother's cat, Junior often fed him, and if I misplaced it, he would know where it was.

Junior looked over at Senior for permission to address me. With a stoic, nonchalant face, Senior kept looking at the TV and said, "Lucky's gone."

Sheer panic struck my body, and emotions flooded my eyes with tears. In a breach of the otherwise decorum I had with my father, I yelled out, "What do you mean Lucky's gone?"

Senior leaped off the chair and charged me like a mad bull. In some magical way, Mama interceded between us. He looked Mama square in the eye and said, "Move, Jean. I'm gonna handle this."

Mama, equipped with some celestial power, refused to move and charged him, asking, "What do you mean Lucky's gone? Mike, what did you do to this boy's cat?"

My heart started pounding in my chest.

"Well, you said get rid of Sheila. She was an attack dog. She needed some type of bait. So we took Lucky and released Lucky at the Hallwood Plaza and then released Sheila. That's the only way to get Sheila away—she needed to chase something. I lost a dog today, and you lost a cat. I don't think she made it." He chuckled and returned to his seat, immediately becoming engaged with the TV show.

Hearing those words and envisioning my beloved white cat being scared out of her mind across a parking lot on the north side of Flint—mind you, not too far from where we were at my auntie's house—being chased by vicious Sheila, made my legs give out and my heart almost stopped. I didn't have very many things that I could truly love, and that would love me back. But Lucky was one of those animals that gave me joy.

My mother consoled me the best she could, but she knew that if she didn't get dinner ready, this situation was going to become worse. I sat there in a corner and cried. Senior turned the TV up to drown out my tears.

I woke up from this memory abruptly, startled, sweat pouring down my face, my body stuck to the leather couch in Dr. Reed's office.

I gotta get out of here.

But Dr. Reed assuages my fear. "No, Mario, we must dig deeper. We must start pulling these off, layer by layer."

I struggle, getting up, disoriented, confused. I don't want these memories anymore. I don't want this pain. I don't want to ever go through this again. I've been through this. I've lived this. I'm not a victim. I'm a survivor.

She calms me down, gives me something to drink, and guides me back to the couch. And ushers me into even more memories.

Memory: The Human Punching Bag

I arrive at a memory that sets the tone for me and Junior's relationship, even to this day.

"Just stay in there. Don't move. If you move, I'm gonna whoop your ass," Senior orders, as I stand in his dungeon—the garage where he built an arena for the dog fights. The stench of feces, urine, dogs, sweat, and blood always permeated that floor. It was me and Junior's job the next day to go in and clean the walls of the dog fight pen and clean up the floors. No matter how much we scrubbed, no matter how many times we sanitized, it still reeked. The wood that confined the dogs into the pens was utterly stained with blood and dog remains, as if the very stench was caused by the demonic spirits that were involved in these fights.

I stand there tight, and I close my eyes because I know what's coming next.

Junior's fist connects with my face, and I fall back into the wall.

"That's right, son. You knocked the hell out of him. Now hold your form tight when you hit. Throw with your right hand."

I shake it off. I'm beginning to be able to take a punch very easily—probably not the goal of an eight-year-old.

Several more blows land on my face.

"OK, now you gotta work on your body blows also."

Now, as a chunky child, this part never felt good. People think that fat provides a cushion, but it doesn't. Several more body blows hit me, and then he said, "OK, Junior, that's enough."

I curl up on the floor, gasping for air, looking out the corner of my eyes as Senior and Junior walk to the other side of the garage, leaving me lying on the ground. Senior is coaching Junior on how to punch better.

Yes, you read that correctly: He used me as a punching bag so that his oldest son could learn how to fight.

I remember the first time this happened, and I thought I was going to have my turn next. But I was told that I wasn't allowed to hit him back.

I got up off the floor, and Senior offered me the same threat he did each time: "Don't tell nobody what happened here. If you do, I'm going to kill your mother."

That threat alone silenced me even into my adult life.

If Mama ever asked—and she would—I was to say that we got into a fight. Not that he was using me as a punching bag for Junior.

The memory fades, and I'm back in Dr. Reed's office, tears streaming down my face.

"How could we ever have a brother relationship when the dynamics of our relationship have always been abuse, superiority, and neglect?" I ask her, my voice breaking. "Family members used to always say that I picked on Junior. Because from their limited standpoint, when we weren't at the house, whenever Junior stepped out of line and Senior wasn't around to stop me, I took every opportunity I had to whoop his butt. I mean unmercifully. I would pick up a weapon—whether it be a brick or stick—and I would go upside his head. Because his precious father wasn't around to protect him, and I didn't have to stand there and take it."

Dr. Reed nods, understanding the complexity of what I'm describing.

"It was selective outrage, selective concern coupled with half-truths and no love that utterly bothered me. I began putting up walls at a very young age when I began to witness these types of things. No one could ignore the scars, the wounds. I was a child who sometimes felt like I was being tortured daily, who felt like I was being beaten sometimes to within an inch of my life. I was a child who endured many things that my family knew, and they chose to do nothing."

I look at Dr. Reed, searching her face for answers I know she doesn't have.

"So how can I embrace them? How can we move forward as some big, happy family when I'm expected to feel like a necessary or some interchangeable being within the family? When my worth is secondary to a dog? When in the absence of a dog, I'm the one chained in the basement and beaten?"

But Dr. Reed isn't done with me yet. She guides me deeper, to a memory that makes everything else pale in comparison.

It was an otherwise normal day at the house—as if anything we experienced had any semblance of normalcy. Me and Junior had an opportunity to sit and watch TV. Tensions had been brewing all day in the house but not like they normally did. This day felt different. This time Mama was upset about some lipstick that she found in Senior 's car.

Now mind you, me and Junior both knew that Senior had another woman. He took us to her house while we were driving around. But this chick left her lipstick in his car, and Mama found it.

She pressed him and pressed him and pressed him about it, questioning him ceaselessly. He tried numerous times to walk away and argue back, but Mama was upset.

A normal person, when hearing this type of discord, would try to stop it. But it was so normal for us that we continued watching TV.

But then there was a turn. Mama ended up pushing Senior too much. After a couple of slaps, we turned to see what scarred me even to this day.

Senior grabbed Mama by her hair and yanked her to the other side of the house and closed the door behind them. He yelled back, "Don't come in here."

Banging against the walls. Mama saying, "No, Mike. Please, Mike, don't do it, Mike." He never responded. All we kept hearing was banging.

I wanted to see what was going on. Even Junior was trying to peer in. Then we heard the door to their bedroom close. All we kept hearing through the walls was smacks and punches. And as usual, it went silent.

Later, storming through the house was Senior in an absolute rage, knocking things off the counter, going to the sink, blood across his face, scratches on his arms, cussing, threatening to go back and give her some more since she cut him.

In one swift move, he slaps me when he sees me, grabs his keys, and storms out the door.

I nursed my cheek, but curiosity peaked, and I wanted to see what I heard.

We had an L-shaped hallway—no windows, no pictures, just a long L-shaped hallway that connected the dining room to the two bedrooms on the other side of the house. When I flicked the light switch on the hall wall, I could see blood. Circular patterns of blood and handprints of blood all throughout the walls. It looked like he ran her head into every wall all the way down to their bedroom.

There was blood on the carpets, on the walls.

We walked into the room, and Mama was sprawled out on the floor, unconscious.

I shook her, then looked at my hands and saw they were covered in blood.

What happened next was some kind of blur. Senior came back and ordered us to clean the whole hallway, much like we did with the dogs. I remember scrubbing the walls and sobbing, not knowing the condition of my mother, thinking that each time the towel went into the bucket and came out red, this was my mother's blood that was going into the mop pail.

Somehow—I believe because his brother and friends were police officers—they made it look like Mama got into a fight with someone in the neighborhood or she was attacked. She got sent to the hospital for several days.

We were not allowed to go to the hospital to see her. We had to go stay with relatives for a couple of days until Mama was able to come out of the hospital.

When Mama left the hospital and came home, our relationship and the household was never the same. She became more cold and disconnected. I could literally feel in the house that one day, someone was going to die.

She moved more calculatedly. If you could actually touch hate, I believe it was palpable in our house. She hated him at this moment.

I learned later that she was pregnant during this time and lost the baby.

I open my eyes at Dr. Reed's office, and she's crying. A tear streaks down her face as she tries to remain professionally composed, but her face betrays her.

I've always felt bad talking to people about things that happened to me. I'm a talker—I like to talk—so I don't talk to get sympathy, but I hate it when my memories make someone cry.

"The way that I was raised made me feel like this was what I deserved," I tell her, my voice barely above a whisper. "I'm a logical person. If everyone found me so unlovable, if everybody hated me, if everybody around me didn't want me around them, then there must be something about me that warranted it. So treating me bad and hurting me felt like that's what should happen. That's what you do to Mario."

Dr. Reed wipes her eyes and leans forward. "Mario, that little boy didn't deserve any of that. None of it. What happened to you wasn't love—it was torture."

"But it's all I knew," I whisper. "When people hurt me, at least I knew they saw me. When they ignored me, I disappeared completely."

"That's why you chase people who can't love you properly," she says, her voice gentle but firm. "That's why you accept crumbs and call it a feast. That's why you think love is supposed to hurt. Because you were taught that pain and attention were the same thing."

I nodded, understanding flooding through me like a dam breaking.

"The Unrequited Lover, your family, even your relationship with yourself—you're still that little boy cleaning up blood and thinking it's your fault it got spilled."

She's right. I've been carrying that little boy around my whole life, letting him make decisions about love based on lessons learned in a house of horrors.

"It's time to tell that little boy he's safe now," Dr. Reed says. "It's time to teach him what real love looks like. Love doesn't leave bruises. Love doesn't make you clean up its messes. Love doesn't use your body as a punching bag for someone else's education."

For the first time in my life, I began to understand that maybe—just maybe—I've been looking for love in all the wrong ways because I was taught all the wrong lessons about what love means.

Maybe it's time to learn a new definition.

Maybe it's time to stop expecting love to hurt. The little boy who cleaned up his mother's blood from those hallway walls learned that love and violence lived in the same house. But the man sitting in this office is learning that real love doesn't leave bruises, doesn't make you a target, doesn't confuse your pain with its passion. It's going to take time to unlearn what that little boy was taught. But for the first time, I believe it's possible.

Chapter 6: The Crumbs They Called Love

I enter Dr. Reed's office with apprehension, considering our last meeting. I know that reliving and revisiting these memories is part of the process, but I'm not too certain this is where I want to go. Apprehension and fear clench my chest so hard that I wonder if this is truly what I need in my life.

I enter her office, and she's sitting there in picturesque professionalism. Hair tied in a neat bun, traditional black glasses, power suit, pen and pad in hand, waiting for me and welcoming me.

I sit down on my usual spot on the couch. I think, *"Hi, dear friend, long time no see."* I'm such a clown sometimes.

Dr. Reed locks eyes with me, and for a brief moment, her eyes empower me. It's weird. Her eyes used to be mirrors to me—when I looked at her, they would always reflect something in me that I didn't want but needed to see. But today, her eyes seem to echo power and encouragement.

I'm all committed until we start talking.

"Welcome, Mario. I know we've had some rough sessions, but I think we're getting to the root issues here. In today's session, I want to dive a little deeper, but I want it to be more organic. I want you to sail the ship to where your thoughts lie. We've talked a lot about Senior, but I can't help but feel like there's more to what's going on."

I squirm on the couch slightly. She quickly notices and makes notes on that dreaded pad of hers. One day I'm gonna sneak a peek at what she's writing down.

"That memory of Christmas struck a chord with you. It seems like holiday seasons mean a lot to you, which I struggle to understand considering some of the scenarios you've told me."

I responded, "It always seemed like during the holidays, most times we were on our best behavior—which were far and few in between, if at all. It seemed like this was a time when we came together and enjoyed each other. Well, most of them," I say as I scratch my hand and look away.

Dr. Reed leans forward sharply and points at me sternly. "There. Right there."

I paused and look around. *Right there where?* I wonder, then verbalize it. "Right there where?"

"You had a memory or thought. Let's explore that. Whatever that was is another brick in this wall that we need to tear down."

Memory: Christmas Fun with Chevon

It was a cold, snowy Christmas morning. It was one of our first Christmases without Senior in the home. It was nice for him not to be there, but I couldn't help but notice it didn't feel and look the same.

Senior made a nice sum of money working at General Motors. Outside of Mama's random jobs here and there, he was the breadwinner. So, this Christmas didn't have the flair of our previous ones.

We still had a tree, which Mama always loved to spray with fake snow. The usual late '80s/early '90s colors of red, green, white, and silver adorned the tree. But what was vastly different was what was under the tree. There were sparse gifts under the tree—not the usual onslaught of gifts that were bought to assuage the fear and abuse we endured.

I could almost guess what was in some of those boxes because I was there when she got them. I knew that within some of those boxes were jogging suits from Old Newsboys, some cologne, and toys from the Salvation Army. We didn't have the money to splurge on gifts. Hell, we were barely able to keep a roof over our heads.

Senior left Mama with the sole responsibility of paying all the bills—the mortgage, car note, food, and having money for other expenses around the house. This was beyond the salary of someone who worked as a cashier at Sears.

In the early stages of their divorce, it was up to him to pay child support and alimony, which most of the time he refused to pay. This month was no different.

At this time in our life, we survived off grace, pity, food stamps, and soup kitchens. Mama was able to throw some food together for Christmas dinner, which I was thankful for.

During the last couple of years, we typically went to my maternal grandmother's house for the holidays. This brought mixed feelings for me. Sometimes family can be such a blessing, but then there are times when you can be made to feel like a total outsider, even amongst family—sometimes even unwelcome.

My maternal grandmother made it very clear that my brother and I were the least of her favorite grandchildren. Even today, I still don't understand why that was, but she definitely made differences between us and even in the treatment between her own children.

It almost seemed to me that Mama didn't care or didn't let it bother her. It was as if she'd come to accept it and welcome any attention her mother would give her. I've learned in life not to fight too hard with people, specifically if I need something from them.

Although my maternal grandmother's food wasn't the best, it was a free meal. Instead of scrambling around our house for something to eat, at the very least I could get some reasonable food.

Mama mentioned that for this holiday, we were going to stop at the soup kitchen on the way to Granny's house. She had to figure out a ride for us to get to the other side of town.

This was a point in life that I hated—our reliance on the kindness of strangers. It never sat right with me. It was almost like a bond of entrapment, an unspoken quid pro quo: If I help you do this, what am I going to get in return?

We arrive at the soup kitchen and get in line for food. It reminds me of an assembly line at a manufacturing plant where everything is lined up and very mechanical. It's rather depressing to be in there, to be honest. Hordes of people waiting, various questionable smells, the look of pity on so many people's faces, and the apathetic look of some of the employees/volunteers.

I never understood why you would do this job if you didn't have a heart for the people. *Have you ever considered how hard it is for some people to swallow their pride? To take handouts? To come here in this weather? To some people, this may be the only meal they get this week. And you look as if they're bothering you, always frustrated.*

I get my rectangular container that's sectioned off and walk through the assembly line to get my portion of food. The food isn't that bad—nothing like my mother's cooking, definitely not like my paternal grandmother's. I swear that woman had the Hands of God in the kitchen. I've never had a meal from her that wasn't absolutely delicious.

We scarf down the food and are met by my godsister Chevon. Whenever she's around, I know that trouble isn't too far away, but I love her.

This memory invokes so much raw emotion within me. The memory of my godsister has always been one of turmoil for me—one that life has taught me a lesson about valuing the time we have:

Chevon eventually disappeared and reappeared in my life years later. We couldn't be more brother and sister if we were actually born blood. We rekindled our relationship, which was never broken. I was teaching a Zumba class at the time, and she would come and learn. One day we got into a heated exchange via text message, and when I saw her, she tried to talk to me. In true stubborn Mario fashion, I didn't want to hear her, and I walked away. Had I known what was going to happen the next month, I would have embraced her, hugged her as tight as I could, and possibly never let her go. A month later, her truck was discovered abandoned on the side of the road with blood inside it, but no sign of her. Years have gone by with no trace of her. I mourn her to this day.

Chevon comes in but doesn't eat. She sits with us and jokes and talks. Her mother greets my mother, and they sit and talk and gossip as they usually would.

Chevon gets up and says, "Y'all come with me."

We go to our mothers and tell them we're gonna go ahead and walk around downtown. Mama, barely even acknowledging us, waves us off and tells us to meet her at Granny's house.

We walk around downtown, and Chevon tells us to go into Citizens Bank Hall because they had a party there. Being the youngest of the trio, I went along with her.

We sneak into the building and start walking around. Lo and behold, there's an entire empty buffet room. It looks like they're taking down the buffet from some ritzy get-together. There's all kinds of food that I can't identify, but I eat it.

One of the desserts makes me fall in love with it all over again. I can't identify it then—I know what it is now—but it's some flaky pastry with nuts and sugar and stickiness that I inhale as much as I can. It takes me years to find out what it is, but it's called baklava, and it's truly not the chef's kiss, but the God's kiss of desserts.

As we're stuffing our faces with food, we hear rumblings coming from the backroom and hallway. We ran and hid behind a curtain wall, peering out to see security looking around. The security guard, suspicious, exits the ballroom.

After a few minutes, we run out, and as we're running, the building cleaners see us and yell, "Hey, what are you doing here?"

With my mouth full of baklava and hands sticky, I run down the stairs while Junior tries to catch an elevator. I look at him and shake my head, knowing I'm getting out of there. Catching my vibe, he runs down the stairs with me. Chevon doesn't wait for anybody—she gets out of there!

With our bellies full and having escaped security, we stroll down the streets of downtown Flint. It's nice to be out there sometimes. Holiday lights were displayed on the street poles and a lot of downtown Flint streets were constructed of recycled bricks as opposed to pavement, providing a more rustic, authentic look.

There's hardly any traffic, and no people, so we walked around looking at the various buildings, talking and laughing.

I remember that it started to snow, and we made it to downtown Flint near a pavilion that hadan ice rink. I remember standing there as the snow was falling, trying to catch some on my tongue, taking in the serene scene of this Christmas, not knowing that my joy and peace will be short-lived.

We looked down the road and saw the twelve-story high-rise that my grandmother stayed in. We knew that today's menu would be dressing, which she makes spicy and non-spicy. Very weirdly, she puts hard-boiled eggs in her dressing. I still don't understand that today. There was also potato salad (not as good as my mother's—she loves mustard in potato salad, and my grandmother uses a lot), overcooked chicken, ham, and shade and family drama.

Chevon, knowing she won't be welcome, walks us toward the building. We hug each other, and Junior and I buzz grandmother's apartment on the seventh floor.

In true form of feeling unwanted, someone answers: "Who is it?"

"Mario and Junior," we respond.

No response, just a buzz to come up.

What feels like hours later, the elevator comes, and with each ding, I know we're getting closer and closer to a place I don't particularly want to be, but I have to be.

Although we're the poorest in the family, we still have a house—a substantial house with three bedrooms, two bathrooms, breezeway, and a two-car garage. No food, but we have a bigger space. But we never have family over to our house. No one offers or wants to come to our house. So, for these types of holidays, we cram ourselves into Granny's one-bedroom apartment. There's about fifteen to twenty people scattered throughout the apartment.

Granny isn't an intimidating woman in stature at all, but the fact that I rarely remember even seeing her smile goes to show her personality. She sits there all four-foot-ten in height—if she's 100 pounds, I'd be surprised—supervising everyone.

"Go in there and wash your hands," she orders as we give her a hug. No welcome, just a half-hearted hug. *Typical.*

We wash our hands as ordered and go to the kitchen to get some food. I can feel Grandmother's peering eyes burning at the back of my head.

"Now y'all make sure y'all get some bread and some vegetables. Y'all not gonna dog out the meat. Y'all hear me? Other people gotta eat."

We turn and acknowledge almost in unison: "Yes, ma'am."

I stand there thinking: *Aren't* we *the other people who need to eat?* But I dare not say this. I already know drama is going to be started by someone, but it's not going to be me.

We exit the kitchen with our plates in hand and are greeted by Mama, who is probably on her fourth or fifth drink.

"Where y'all been at?" she asks.

I give her a puzzled look. *You really don't remember?* Then, as if it hits her: "I hope y'all didn't get in no trouble. Go in there and eat. There's some room on the balcony."

The balcony? *In* wintertime? *In* Flint? I just look and keep moving. Her drinking at this point is out of control.

I never fully understand one thing about my family. We have family get-togethers knowing everyone has children, but they never think of creating an atmosphere for children. The bar is in full flow, the heat set on the second circle of hell, there's loud blues music, and half a dozen side conversations. The kids are relegated to grandmother's bedroom, but due to the size of the apartment, several other adults take up space in that room too, drinking and talking. We can't even enjoy wrestling on TV because of everything that's going on.

There are times when I can almost set my clock to when something is about to hit the roof. It could be any household I walk into, but I feel in the atmosphere that in less than a few minutes, something is about to go off. To be honest, I welcome it. It's good to see other people get into it from our perspective—some drama that I don't have to be involved with. Bring it on!

I'm not sure what breaks the camel's back, but all I remember is hearing a whole bunch of swearing and yelling coming from the living room. I peer around the corner and watch as my uncle and his girlfriend argue with his younger sister.

Not only can I predict that there's going to be an issue, I can sometimes even predict the players. Even today, I always ask who's going to be there whenever I go to an event because I can determine, based upon who's going to be there, the kind of vibes and potential situations that could arise. Mixing alcohol with some of these people with unspoken drama, pent-up childhood traumas, and liquor all spells trouble.

I remember standing there—fingers in faces, yelling, hands being extended. Mama, being the oldest, always tries to keep the peace and interjects herself to try to smooth out the situation. I'm not sure why she got involved because we all know that Senior was the only one who could push Ms. Emma Jean around. The second anybody touches or approaches her wrong, all hell is gonna break loose.

I remember this happening in slow motion: As my mother tries to separate the parties, someone's hand goes in Mama's face. My inner child grabs a bowl of popcorn, pulls up a chair, and sits to watch what's about to occur.

The immediate snake-like reaction of my mama swatting that hand out of her face and fully inserting herself into the drama. She starts yelling and cussing everybody out.

I hear my grandmother saying: "All right, Jean, it's time for you to go. It's time for you to go."

As if she's the primary antagonist who started this! It's how it always feels in my family—that she or anybody associated with her is always in the wrong, and the younger siblings are always right.

Mama snatches her purse and says, "That's fine. Mario, Junior, let's go."

Several adults decide it's time for them to leave too.

I didn't get a chance to get no dessert or take-home plate.

Snap! Snap!

Dr. Reed breaks me from my recollection. "Wow. You have interesting family dynamics."

Interesting is an understatement.

"I can see that your holidays were a mixture of highs and lows."

"Yeah," I sheepishly agreed.

"You don't talk about your grandmother very much. Or any other family members."

I looked at her; my head tilted to the side. "What's to tell?" I say.

She looks at me as if she can peer into my soul. "Are you sure there's nothing you want to talk about?"

"No. What more can I talk about? I don't truly understand what it is to be a family because the one that I have either doesn't want me or acts like they don't want me. It's not something I care to talk about, or I think is even relevant."

"Why don't you feel like a member of your family?"

I counter her a little more forcefully than necessary: "I think the question should be: Why don't they want me? I didn't do anything to them people."

I thought that comment would have taken her aback, but she remains extremely poised.

"All families have some kind of dysfunction. You must work through that dysfunction to find, for lack of a better term, your sweet spot."

It's like trying to find a sweet spot in a pile of shit. But I refrain from stating that.

"I remember you stating that you used to stay with her. Let's talk about that."

Memory: The House Fire

I remember being thirteen or fourteen and having our home destroyed due to our inability to financially afford the house that we had. With Senior not providing Mama routine financial support, she couldn't afford to keep the insurance on the house. Unfortunately, one of the people who used to stay with us burnt the electrical wires in the ceiling, which caused a fire.

I remember coming home that day and getting off the bus. Usually, all kinds of parents were at the bus stop waiting to retrieve their children, and we knew most of them. My mother was never there because our house was literally around the corner, and it didn't make much sense. She tried a couple times, and I let her know: "We're big kids; we don't need you picking us up from the bus stop."

When we got off the bus, we were immediately greeted by several kids and concerned looks from almost all the adults.

"Oh my God, did you know your house burned down?"

I was like, "What? What are you talking about?"

Another little boy: "Yeah, your house is burnt. What are you gonna do?"

I forgot how tacky kids can be.

We rush around the corner to see our house in complete destruction and Mama standing outside in tears.

"What happened?" I ask.

"The roof caught fire. Everything inside is ruined," she says, like this is the last ounce of strength she could muster. "It's all gone."

We were homeless.

As I reflect on this memory, it's important to note that during this time, I cannot independently recall seeing any family members around to help.

During this time, we jumped from house to house. We stayed in a seedy hotel in downtown Flint called the Berridge Hotel. It was a very low-rent building. I remember pulling up there. *So, this is home now?*

It was almost like they didn't even want to mask the fact that this place was frequented by prostitutes and their tricks. All kinds of drug addicts stayed here. I remember walking through hallways that reeked of urine and weed. I remember walking into the room, and there was one king-size bed and a cot. Mama advised that we were all going to have to stay there together.

This was one of the lowest points for us.

We had to sneak back into the house to try and salvage any clothing that we could. They roped it off as condemned because it was unsafe for human habitation. We didn't have our car—Mama lost it months ago because she couldn't afford to pay the bills. She ultimately lost her job too.

The only things we had were what we could fit inside book bags, and we were able to get free bus passes from the Red Cross.

One weekend, we were able to hop on a bus and go over to my mama's sister's house on the north side of Flint. I was happy to go see my cousins and some of the family members. We went inside her house and got in front of the fan to cool off because it was so hot from the bus and the walking we had to do. She had relatively new furniture.

She reprimanded me: "You stink. Do not sit on my new furniture. Go outside and sit on the porch," she ordered in disgust.

I admit I was probably sweaty from the heat, but what I needed at that time was compassion and reprieve from the heat. *We were already at our lowest, so why kick us when we're down? Why state such negative things toward me?*

Feeling dejected, I went to sit on the porch. It was too hot to feel much like playing. I remember sitting out there with several of my other cousins when Grandmother was there. She asked several of my cousins to walk with her.

I didn't mind because it was hot, and I remember Junior walking out and looking down the street as they were walking and saying, "She's getting them ice cream."

Me and a couple of my other cousins sat up. I was like, "What?"

Lo and behold, down the street was the ice cream man, and she was buying her favorite grandchildren ice cream while the rest of us sat there.

They went around the block, and within fifteen to twenty minutes came back with no trace of evidence that they were eating ice cream. I guess it was a ploy to walk down the street and around the corner so the other kids wouldn't see.

I remember my other cousin, whose brother went with Grandmother, told his mother, who reached in her pocket to pull out some money.

"Y'all go get y'all some ice cream," she said.

That was my Aunt Angie—always the voice of reason, always the one who would call out the injustice within the family. She gave me a dollar to go get some ice cream, but pride took hold of me. I don't know if it was so much pride as it was sadness that this is how they did things in my family. It didn't make sense to me. There was no point in telling Mama because it had become clear that that's how her mother was.

There was nothing more I could say or do at that time, so I sat back and waited for it to be time for us to get on the last bus and head back to the hotel.

What eventually ended up happening was Mama had to go into a shelter. Junior was shipped off to Job Corps because he wasn't doing what he was supposed to do in school. I wasn't allowed to go to the shelter with Mama because of age requirements—I could only go to the men's shelter, and there were safety concerns with someone my age being there with lecherous old men.

It was decided without my input that I would go stay at my mama's youngest sister's house. That was okay, but I knew I would have to walk on pins and needles in that house.

Before Mama dropped me off and before her entry into the shelter—which I didn't know meant I wouldn't routinely see her—she grabbed me by my shoulders, gave me a hug, looked me in the eye, and said: "You know how your auntie can be. Just be good, and I promise I'll come see you. We're gonna get a nice, new, beautiful home when I get out of here."

Tears flooded my eyes, and I watched as my mother hopped into the cab and departed, not knowing that there would be a significant amount of time before I actually saw her again.

For weeks, I stayed at this house feeling like a slave and an unwanted guest. There was always the precipice of an argument with her or being talked about. It was nice when she went to work because I didn't have to deal with the attitude, but when she came home, it was like a tornado hit that house.

One day, she came home, and I was sitting inside watching TV. I liked TV. We didn't have cable where I was staying, so the fact that she had cable—although it was illegal cable that she paid the local crackhead to install—was enjoyable.

She walked in: "What are you doing in here? All the other kids are outside. Get out so I can clean my house," she snapped.

I started getting up. She rushed over, snatched the remote, turned it off, and headed to the kitchen.

I sat on the porch and stared off into nothingness. Her two other kids were playing around in the front, and I'm sitting next to her oldest son. She commands him to come into the house and begins to yell at him about his bed not being made.

He told her: "Ma, I wasn't even in here. Mario was the one laying in that bed."

She yelled loud enough for me to hear: "Next time, tell Mario to take his fat ass outside and not mess up your bed."

That hurt. Yes, I was on the chunky side, and the "fat ass" comment was heavily emphasized when she was talking.

He came outside, closed the door, looked at me, and I gave him that look like "I know."

Then he said, "Man, she's trippin'. Come on, let's roll to the park."

Several days later, I was so discouraged with the way things were progressing. I overheard phone conversations with her complaining to one of her friends: "Yeah, girl, I got him over here with me. Jean ain't sent no money for him either. He think he's gonna eat me out of house and home? Better think again."

She would make separate meals for her kids and have me eat bologna or something of that nature. I didn't mind—I was used to it.

One morning, as I had to get up and go to my summer job—which I was happy to get so I could get some money—I was so upset I saw a bottle of pills in her cabinet. I took several of them and left the house.

Walking down Detroit Street heading toward Carpenter Road, I remember euphoria passed over me, and everything started spinning and spinning. Then crash—I fell to the ground.

I lay there for what seemed like forever. No car stopped. No one checked on me. I'm not even sure how, but after a while, I crawled to the payphone and called my aunt to ask if she could pick me up because I'd passed out.

She reluctantly showed up with no concern. I didn't tell her what was going on. She commented: "You gotta lose some weight. That's why you passed out—all that fat around your heart. It's not good."

I asked her if it was possible for me to go stay with my grandmother.

She laughed: "You think it's gonna be better at her house? I know you're not happy here, but good luck. Go ahead and pack your stuff up."

She called my grandmother, and the agreement was for me to go stay with her.

Staying with my grandmother was what I expected—many lows, very few highs.

The first day was okay. Again, this was a one-bedroom apartment, so clearly, I was gonna be sleeping on the floor in the living room. But she had so many rules. Like if it was raining and thundering, all electricity had to go off, and it was bedtime because of the danger. One day it stormed around 4:00, and she told me to turn off everything, including the fan—mind you, it was warm outside—and to make my pallet on the floor and go to bed. I wasn't allowed to sleep on the furniture.

When it got dark outside, I was expected to have my teeth brushed, showered, and be in bed before 10:00.

The following days exemplified how unwelcome I was at her house. Remember, I had to be in bed before 10:00, but she would often leave and forget that I didn't have a key to the apartment. I would have to wait for her to show up.

I was staying in her apartment in downtown Flint and went to school at Beecher High School, so I had to take a bus to get there. I had to get up early in the morning, about 6:00, to get ready to be on the 7:00 bus. I often didn't make it back from school until 4:00.

Some days she would be out with her friends or wherever—most of the time I didn't know where. She would show up about 7:00 or 8:00 with no explanation.

One night still haunts me: She didn't show up until almost 9:00 that night. I remember sitting alone in the parking lot playground at a school called Doyle-Ryder, a fourteen-year-old boy with nowhere to go and no one who cared where he was.

From the swing set, I could see her apartment building—seven stories of brick and broken dreams. Every twenty to thirty minutes, like some desperate ritual, I would drag myself off that swing, walk across the empty parking lot to her building, and press her apartment number on the intercom. My finger would linger on that button, hoping against hope that I would hear her voice, that she would answer, that she was home and I could finally get inside.

But there was only silence. Always silence.

I would walk back to that swing set, my stomach empty, my heart emptier, and wait some more. Cars would drive by, and I would look up hopefully, thinking maybe this time it would be her. Maybe this time someone would come for me.

But no one ever came.

The sun set. The streetlights came on. Other kids my age were at home having dinner with their families, doing homework, feeling safe and loved. And I was sitting on a swing in the dark, wondering if I would have to sleep outside, wondering if anyone in the world cared whether I lived or died.

At around 9:00 PM, I happened to look up and see that her bedroom light was finally on. My heart jumped—not with joy, but with relief so profound it almost made me sick. She was home. I wouldn't have to sleep in the parking lot. I wouldn't have to figure out how to survive another night alone.

The rules of the apartment building were that no one could buzz you in past 8:00 PM, so I already knew it was gonna be an issue getting in because the odds that she would want to walk down seven flights without an attitude were slim to none.

I approached the building, and one of her friends, Jackie, whose apartment I sometimes stayed in waiting for Grandmother to come home, happened to be in the vestibule. She let me in, and I was able to get up to my grandmother's apartment.

I remember knocking on the door, and she opened it. I gave her an inquiring look with my eyes. *Where have you been?*

As usual, no response. No greeting, no, "Hey grandbaby, I'm sorry, where you been at?" Nothing. Not a care in the world.

I walked in, and she was cooking and had one of her male friends, David, at the table. I was exceptionally hungry because I didn't have any money and I'd sat outside in the heat for several hours.

I went to the bathroom to get ready for bed. When I got out, I noticed she'd prepared food for her and David, and there was nothing left for me.

Sensing my frustration, she said dismissively: "If you want something to eat, fetch something from the fridge."

She and David resumed eating their meal, drinking, laughing, and playing loud music.

I stood in the kitchen with two pieces of bread and a couple slices of bologna, scarfed that down, and was ready to go lay down.

I was wondering when this makeshift blues concert and gin-and-juice room situation that was going on in the living room would resolve itself so I could lay down, but to no avail. It continued.

By 10:00, I was laying on my pallet and covered my head with the sheet as music blasted in the background. Less than five feet from me was Grandmother, her boyfriend, and a couple more people at the table drinking and laughing.

As I lay there on the floor, I could see the patio door. I was existing instead of sleeping. This went on for a couple hours, maybe until midnight, and I had to get up at 6:00 again to redo this day.

During this time, my mother was MIA. She happened to show up at Grandmother's house one day and was shocked to see me there.

"Boy, what are you doing here?" she asked.

"I've been here for a couple months. I couldn't take it where I was," I said, tears filling my eyes.

I tried to explain to her what was going on, and she cut me off and said that in a few more months, the program she was in would be done, and we would be able to get a house.

I walked her down to what I thought was the street so I could see her off, but she had one of her boyfriends, Earl, waiting for her. Several other friends were in the van.

She got in the car, grabbed her drink, started laughing, and they drove off.

I don't know when I'm gonna see her again. Nice that she was enjoying her life, hanging with her friends, and having a good time.

Junior was away at Job Corps, making new friends and making a better life for himself.

During this time, Mario had only Mario. I had no peace, no quiet, no money, no home, no family. And at that time, no hope.

I open my eyes in Dr. Reed's office, feeling drained and hollow.

"Mario," she says softly, "that little boy was completely alone. Abandoned by everyone who was supposed to protect him."

I nodded, unable to speak for a moment.

"You learned that family was conditional. That love was something you had to earn by being invisible, by not being a burden. That asking for basic needs like food or shelter or attention was 'too much.'"

"But they were all I had," I whisper. "Even when they treated me like shit, they were all I had."

"And that's the trap, isn't it? When the people who abuse you are also the only people you have, you learn to be grateful for crumbs. You learn to call neglect 'normal' and abandonment 'family.'"

Her words hit me like a revelation. I think about grandmother's ice cream favoritism, about being locked out of her apartment, about sleeping on the floor while she partied with her friends. I think about my aunt calling me fat and making me eat bologna while her kids got real meals.

"They trained me to accept less," I say, my voice getting stronger. "They trained me to think I didn't deserve basic human kindness."

"Exactly. And now as an adult, when someone treats you with crumbs—like the Unrequited Lover keeping you in the shadows—it feels familiar. It feels like love because it's the only kind of love you've ever known."

I lean back on the couch, emotionally exhausted but somehow clearer.

"That Christmas with Chevon," I say, "sneaking into that building and eating that baklava—that was the most joy I remember feeling during that whole period. Not because of the food, but because for once, someone included me in something fun. Someone wanted me around."

"And what happened to Chevon breaks your heart even more because she was one of the few people who showed you unconditional love."

Tears start flowing again. "I was so stubborn. I walked away from her over some stupid argument. And now she's gone, and I can never tell her I'm sorry. I can never tell her how much she meant to me."

"Mario, you were a child dealing with trauma and abandonment. You didn't have the tools then to handle conflict in relationships. You were operating from a place of survival, not security."

"But what if—"

"No what-ifs," she interrupts firmly. "What-ifs will drive you crazy. Chevon knew you loved her. That argument didn't erase years of love and connection."

I sit with that for a moment, feeling some of the guilt lift off my chest.

"The thing that gets me most," I continue, "is how Mama drove off that day. She saw me living on the floor of Grandmother's apartment, and she just...left. Got in that van with her friends and her drink and drove away like I wasn't even her son."

"Your mother was fighting her own demons, Mario. Her drinking, her need to 'live her life' after years of abuse—she was trying to survive too. It doesn't excuse leaving you alone, but it helps explain it."

"But I was a kid," I say, my voice breaking. "I was just a kid, and I had nobody. Junior was at Job Corps living his best life. Mama was in the shelter partying with Earl. Senior had been gone for years. And me? I was sleeping on floors, getting locked out of apartments, being called fat, eating bologna while everyone else got real meals."

"And that little boy learned that he didn't matter. That his needs weren't important. That love was something other people got, but not him."

"Yeah," I whisper. "And now I'm thirty-something years old, and I'm still that little boy sitting on the swing set at Doyle-Ryder, waiting for someone to come home and let me in."

Dr. Reed leans forward, her eyes intense. "But Mario, you're not that little boy anymore. You have the power now. You have the choice now.

You don't have to wait on stoops or sleep on floors or accept bologna when you deserve a feast."

"Then why do I keep choosing people who treat me like I'm not worth claiming?"

"Because healing isn't linear. Because you're still learning what healthy love looks like. Because it takes time to unlearn a lifetime of lessons about your worth."

She pauses, then continues. "But look at where you are now. You're in therapy. You're facing these memories. You're starting to understand the patterns. That little boy who had no voice? He's got a voice now. And he's starting to use it."

I think about Toni, about how she fought for me at work. About Dr. Reed, sitting here week after week, helping me untangle years of twisted thinking about love and worth.

"Maybe," I say slowly, "maybe the reason everyone left me wasn't because I wasn't worth staying for. Maybe they left because they were broken too. Maybe their leaving says more about them than it does about me."

"Now you're getting it," Dr. Reed says, a small smile crossing her face. "Your worth isn't determined by other people's capacity to love you properly. Your worth is inherent. It was there when you were that little boy sleeping on the floor, and it's here now."

I sit with that truth, feeling it settle into my bones like a warm blanket.

"The crumbs they called love," I say, "weren't love at all."

"No, they weren't. And now that you know the difference, you get to choose something better. You get to demand something better."

"What if I don't know how?"

"Then we'll learn together. One session at a time. One memory at a time. One choice at a time."

For the first time in weeks, I feel something that might be hope. Not the desperate hope of a child waiting to be rescued, but the steady hope of a man who's starting to rescue himself.

"That little boy deserved so much more," I say.

"Yes, he did. And the man he became deserves more too."

I nodded, feeling the truth of that statement in my core.

Maybe it's time to stop accepting crumbs. Maybe it's time to learn what a feast actually looks like.

Dr. Reed leans back in her chair, and I can see something stirring in her eyes—that look she gets when she's about to drop some spiritual wisdom on me.

"Mario, I want you to think about Psalm 23, verse 5. Do you remember it?"

I shake my head. "Not really."

"'Thou preparest a table before me in the presence of mine enemies.' David wrote that. You understand what that means?"

I look at her expectantly.

"It means God doesn't give you scraps while your enemies watch and laugh. He doesn't hand you bologna while your abusers feast on steak. He prepares a TABLE—a full banquet—right in front of the people who hurt you, the people who said you weren't worth a proper meal."

Her voice is getting stronger, more passionate.

"Your grandmother, your aunt, your family who gave ice cream to other kids while you sat on the porch—they were your enemies in that moment. They were the ones trying to convince you that crumbs were all you deserved. But God? God says, 'No, my child gets a TABLE. My child gets the FULL feast.'"

I feel something stirring in my chest, something that feels like power.

"The Unrequited Lover, keeping you in the shadows while they feast on public love with someone else—that's crumb thinking. That's accepting the bologna sandwich while they eat the full meal. But God is preparing a table for you, Mario. A table where you don't have to hide. A table where love is served openly, abundantly, without shame."

She leans forward, her eyes intense.

"You don't get crumbs at God's table, Mario. You get the feast. You get to sit at the head of the table while the people who tried to starve you watch you being fed like the king you were always meant to be."

I feel tears starting, but they're different this time. Not tears of pain, but tears of recognition.

"Stop settling for bologna when God is preparing filet mignon. Stop accepting shadows when He's got you a place in the full light. Stop taking crumbs when He's laid out a banquet with your name on it."

I sit there, letting her words sink in, feeling something shift deep in my soul.

"I deserve a table," I whisper.

"Say it louder."

"I deserve a table."

"LOUDER!"

"I DESERVE A TABLE!"

"That's right. Not crumbs. Not leftovers. Not whatever they decide to throw your way. A TABLE. Prepared by the Most High God. In the presence of everyone who said you weren't worth it."

For the first time in my life, I understand what it means to know my worth. Not just intellectually, but in my bones, in my spirit, in the very core of who I am.

God has prepared a table for me. I'm done eating off the floor. That little boy who sat on swing sets waiting to be let in, who ate bologna while others got full meals, who was grateful for any crumb of attention—he deserves better. God has prepared a table for me, Dr. Reed said. Not crumbs scattered on the ground, but a feast served with dignity. I'm ready to take my seat.

Chapter 7: When God and Pain Shared the Same Pew

Chirp! Chirp! Chirp! Chirp! Chirp!

The sound pierces through my bedroom window like nature's alarm clock, but instead of one or two birds, it sounds like an entire congregation has gathered outside. Their harmonious symphony rises and falls in perfect rhythm, as if they're conducting their own morning worship service. Some voices high and sweet, others deep and melodic, all blending together in a chorus that seems almost too perfect, too orchestrated.

I lie there listening, wondering if this is some kind of sign. The birds sound so joyful, so free, so... faithful in their daily ritual. They show up every morning without fail, singing their hearts out whether anyone's listening or not.

The irony isn't lost on me. Here these creatures are, praising creation without question, while I'm about to dive into why I've spent most of my adult life running from anything that resembles worship.

With a mixture of apprehension and determination, I prepare for another session with Dr. Reed. So much of our conversations has been centered on healing, development, and spirituality. I'm working on the healing and development portions of my life—both are needed—but one area I know I need help with is spirituality.

I have long since shunned religious gatherings and beliefs. Not because I don't feel that there is a supreme being or some guiding principle that we all should follow in life, but so much of my life has been centered around abuse from the hands of those who carried the Bible within their hearts.

When you've gone through as much as I have, holding onto a belief despite how life is treating you can be very difficult. Especially when my introduction into Christianity was met with such myriad feelings.

Memory: Joining Church

It was a normal Sunday. Mama cooked a big breakfast full of pancakes with crispy edges, bacon, sausage, eggs, and milk. I loved Sunday mornings. I should love them because we were going to church but honestly, we got cooking like this for breakfast only on Sunday mornings. My mother believed wholly that we should always dress in our Sunday best. We dressed as if it was Easter every Sunday—three-piece suits, shined shoes, fresh haircuts.

In looking back, it must have been for appearances because it truly wasn't necessary. But on Sundays, we made it to church for Sunday school and then full Sunday service.

Canaan Baptist Church felt like our family church. Not only did all the Bookers go to that church, but even extended members from my mama's side of the family went there. My family was beloved at this church.

It was nice being around other kids outside of school. We weren't allowed to have friends or go visit other people's houses unless they were relatives, so being at church was a reprieve.

I remember the Sunday School room—dank and cramped. I started learning the Bible, not so much studying it. I would sit slouched down in a chair and listen to the stories. What I loved most about church was the choir, so I was waiting for Sunday School to be over so that we could go to full service.

The layout of the church was very reminiscent of Southern Baptist tradition, equipped with stained glass windows, long wooden pews with red cushions, fans printed with Martin Luther King Jr's face, and a humongous podium for the pastor—the renowned Reverend Duncan.

To the right of the pulpit was the ensemble of the Canaan Baptist choir. My mother, grandmother, and aunt were all choir members.

The choir received a signal from the pastor that it was time to start, and with an air of confidence on her face, I knew that Mama knew a new song was going to be played and she knew it was going to go over very well. It would be a church hit.

It was like fire from Heaven flowed down upon the congregation. The notes from the sopranos to the altos to the tenors floated seamlessly through the sanctuary, and the Spirit began to move in ways that made my five-year-old eyes widen in wonder and fear.

Sister Johnson in the third pew started rocking back and forth, her hands raised high, tears streaming down her face as she whispered, "Thank you, Jesus" over and over. Then suddenly, she let out a shout that seemed to come from somewhere deep in her soul and fell backward into the arms of the ushers, who were always strategically positioned for moments like these.

Brother Williams started speaking in what sounded like a completely different language—rapid, flowing words that I couldn't understand but somehow felt in my chest. "Hallelujah shabala kaya honda sai!" he called out, his voice rising above the choir. The Mothers in the front row started fanning themselves and him with their church fans, nodding and saying, "Yes, Lord! Speak, Holy Ghost!"

Mother Patterson, a large woman who usually sat stoically in her seat, suddenly stood up and began what we called the "holy dance"—not the kind of dancing that was forbidden outside these walls, but a spiritual movement that seemed to come from somewhere beyond her control. Her arms moved like waves, her feet seemed to barely touch the ground, and her whole body swayed to a rhythm only she could hear.

The drummer caught the Spirit and started beating out rhythms that seemed to pulse through everyone's heartbeat. The organ player's hands flew across the keys like he was channeling electricity straight from glory. The entire church seemed to vibrate with an energy that made the hair on my arms stand up.

People were falling out all over the sanctuary now—some caught by the ushers with their white gloves and gentle hands, others just sliding to the floor where they lay trembling and calling on Jesus. The ushers moved through the aisles with their small bottles of oil and paper fans, ministering to those who had been "slain in the Spirit."

And through it all, the choir kept singing, Mama's voice soaring above the rest, her hands clapping to a beat that seemed to be directed by Heaven itself. The entire church had become a symphony of worship—some shouting, some singing, some speaking in tongues, some weeping and worshipping in silence.

Me and Junior would fake like we were catching the Holy Ghost while everybody else was in genuine spiritual commotion, but even our childish mimicry couldn't diminish the real power that was moving through that place.

Often, we went unnoticed, but a stern eye from my grandmother in the choir stand let me know she disapproved and we'd better stop it. *You're supposed to be singing, not paying attention to us.*

She would get my mother's attention and let her know that we were acting up. In rare times when he actually did get caught acting up, I would watch my mother coming from the choir stand and escorting Junior to the basement for "correction"—correction meaning a whooping in church. I never got corrected in church, but Junior got corrected frequently, typically for sleeping during service.

During a rousing sermon from Reverend Duncan, we sat a couple pews behind the coveted first row. The row ahead of us was where the Mothers of the church sat. In the Black church, the Mothers sat with big hats, purses filled with peppermints and butterscotch, and if you listened closely, some gossip.

I loved sitting there because even if they didn't say anything, the looks they gave and the nudges they would give each other told me everything I needed to know about certain members of the church—specifically if a sister wasn't dressing a certain kind of way or if one of the ushers' or deacons' eyes weren't on the Lord.

Mixed in that row was a lady who would always yell out while the pastor was talking: "Sho nuff!" Every time she said it, me and Junior would break out laughing. She was so country that we didn't even learn her name—we called her the "Sho Nuff Lady."

Before Reverend Duncan concluded his sermon, he stated: "Before I close, I feel the Spirit upon me to open up the doors of the church." He directed the deacons to bring up a chair to the front of the church.

"If any of you feel it in your spirit that you need a closer walk with God, if you feel that there is something missing in your life and you want God to be more active in your journey, come on and walk up here."

I don't know what came over me, but those words hit me like a brick wall. I felt this urge in my spirit, this indescribable desire that forced me to get up from my seat, eyes filled with tears.

Without stopping to consider the audience or possible consequences, I left my seat. The next thing I knew, I was standing in front of the church, sitting in that chair.

The church erupted with applause and crying. I remember looking over into the choir stand through tear-stained eyes and seeing them holding my grandmother up as the joy of me joining the church and giving my life over to God overwhelmed her. My mother had her hands clasped over her face, crying and praising the Lord.

I did a good thing. I thought it felt so right. It felt so right on time. Everything that I'd been going through—this love of God, that's what I needed in my life.

Junior got up, walked toward the front of the church, and stood next to me. One of the deacons rushed to put another chair in the front next to me, and the church erupted even further in praise.

Reverend Duncan came and embraced us and was the first one to extend the right hand of fellowship, welcoming us into the Kingdom of the Lord. The leadership of the church came and shook our hands, then followed the deacons, the Mothers, the ushers, the choir, and all the other members of the church.

The outpouring of love was so grandiose. I'd never experienced love and acceptance like I felt at that moment in the church.

My grandmother embraced us tightly and said, "Now if we can get your father into this church, it will bless my soul to have my whole family here."

Although raised in church, Senior never went to church with us. He never made excuses—it was just a matter of fact that he did not go to church. He would eat the breakfast that Mama served and cooked, watch TV, train the dogs, or go to the garage, but church was not on his to-do list.

I couldn't wait to get home and tell him, thinking that maybe he would finally be proud of me for something—even if not for me, but because Junior joined also.

When we got home, we rushed to see Senior in his chair watching TV. I approached him like a servant approaching the throne, begging for a moment of His Honor's time.

I nudged Junior to tell him, and he did.

"Hey, Dad. Me and Mario joined church today."

With the most demented look I have ever seen, he responded: "**You did what?**" His thunderous voice echoed throughout the house.

Junior quickly acquiesced: "Well, Mario joined and I went up there with him."

I shot him a look of betrayal, but I wasn't surprised.

The sheer look of disgust and anger that streaked across Senior's face haunts me today. We locked eyes, and it seemed like a minute lasted ten years.

What I thought would be a joyous moment felt like I had sinned against Senior. Like through some biblical tenet that I was unaware of, me joining the church represented a direct affront to his religion, to his moral compass, to his belief of what his family should do.

It was at that moment that I really felt bad. *I shouldn't have done this.*

"You don't know what you did," he stated firmly and aggressively. "You only did that just to show that you were important. Them people there don't know you, don't care nothing about you. And I bet your mama just ate it up."

I stood there knowing full well I'd better not say anything. I almost felt so afraid that I was going to wet myself, but I had to remain silent.

I remember wanting that feeling and spirit that got me out of my seat at church to save me in this very situation—that spirit to move me from that room to safety or even tell me to go to the bathroom—but nothing came. I stood there waiting on a hit, to be berated or something, but nothing happened. It was a surreal moment. This is one of the few times I can actively remember him being disappointed, but also remember not caring how he felt about me.

It's strange that I've never felt a connection to Senior. Even when my family sat me down at the table and told me that I was adopted and I was not his child, then later denied that the event happened, we never bonded.

My mother would tell stories that even as a child, whenever he touched me, I would cry. How as a child, I would never take a bottle from him. The second he walked into the room, I would cry.

There was nothing that I could do to change it. I felt for him as much as I felt for a total stranger. I wanted his love and approval out of some ceremonial obligation; something bound together by some perceived familial tie. But I didn't need it or want it.

So, his approval, or rather disapproval, didn't matter to me. I stood there out of ritual. When he reengaged with the TV, basically dismissing me, I went on to my room.

I was either five or six when this happened, and this is one of the first memories that I have of church. I guess this wasn't a battle that Mama didn't want to fight because she didn't engage but stayed in the kitchen cooking.

When I was in my early twenties, Mama wanted me to go to this new church that she'd been attending. To my surprise, it had a woman as a pastor. It was called In the Name of Jesus Full Gospel Church.

She would go on and talk about how dynamic the services were and how the pastor would give "Words from God" called prophecies. This was strange to me, so I didn't want to go. But it was a late Friday night, so I acquiesced and went with her.

The church was dated and basic. It was very different from Canaan. But what they lacked in aesthetics, they made up for in might.

Friday night prophecy service felt very ceremonial. The pastor and seven of her ministers stood in the front of the church. There was prayer, hymns, and songs that felt very down-home.

One of the ministers stood up—her name was Evangelist Sterns. She got up and spoke-sang, and her voice was like lightning and thunder mixed together. She spoke with such power and determination, commanding so much attention. I was truly in awe of the service.

That was until they read a Scripture from Proverbs, the third chapter, fifth and sixth verses: "Trust in the Lord with all thy heart and lean not unto thine own understanding. In all thy ways acknowledge Him, and He shall direct thy paths."

That Scripture pulled me into a memory.

Memory within a Memory...Proverbs 3:5-6

I was seven and a half years old. Junior and I were in our room playing and roughhousing. Mama was leaving for work or with one of her friends, so she left us alone with Senior, who was on the other side of the house.

As we were playing, Junior ran into the wall, and a thunderous voice ripped through the house, rupturing the quietness:

"What the hell are you doing? I'm trying to rest! Keep the noise down!"

We stopped playing and sat down and opened up our Bibles to practice our Sunday Easter speeches. Mine was derived from Proverbs, the third chapter, fifth and sixth verses. I remember practicing this and calling my grandmother to read it to her on the phone, and how proud of me she was. She nominated my brother and me to read Scriptures in church for Easter service.

As I was reading and trying to study, Junior kept playing around and threw something that hit me in the head. I got up and started tussling with him, and then what seemed like the house shaking—angry footsteps stormed through the house and ripped open our door.

There was an angry Senior standing there. In his hand was the rubber hose, and he was seething with anger.

"I warned you to keep this noise down."

I recoiled to the other corner of the room since I knew what was about to occur.

Junior told Senior, "Dad, we were studying for Easter speeches."

Unwavering in his anger and frustration: "You weren't studying! You were playing around and then lying on God! I said keep it down. I don't care what you think you're doing," he shot back.

Although Mama and I were his main targets, Junior was not immune from discipline.

I jumped in and said, "No, Dad, we were studying," and showed him the Bible and the Scriptures in an attempt to assuage his anger.

He looked at it and then tossed it onto the bed. His anger rose, and with determined and quick momentum, he swung the rubber hose, which connected across our bodies numerous places and times.

I convulsed on the floor in pain, too hurt to scream. Junior was next to me in equal pain.

He sat on the bed and looked at us: "That's a taste of what's gonna happen if you can't recite these so-called speeches verbatim."

I was confident—I'd been studying all week. I remember calling my grandmother to read them.

With snot and tears running down my face, the places where the rubber hose connected starting to swell, it proved very difficult to try to recite Scripture. It was difficult between the sniffles and whimpering and touching all the bruises.

When doing homework, mistakes equaled beatings. If I messed up one line, it was over.

I barely made it five words in, and I started drawing a blank. The next thing I remember was being yanked up and thrown on the bed with Junior and then being beaten repeatedly with the rubber hose.

After he was done, he yelled at me to re-read the Scriptures: "When I come back later, you better know them. If not, you'll get another beating."

I remember sitting on the ground as teardrops soiled the Scriptures as I read Proverbs, third chapter, fifth and sixth verses.

This was when I began to equate pain, blood, and the Bible. It was my last memory of me reading the Bible.

I snap back to the present. Mama looks at me like she's seeing a ghost. She looks perplexed as to why I have such a reaction.

It made no sense for me to tell her what my heart bears, but I ran from church and swore I'd never return.

However, upon leaving the church, I could not dismiss the familiar sense of longing for belonging that first arose when I joined the congregation at age five. I couldn't shake it despite this walk down memory lane.

I needed to come back. Maybe I could get that old feeling back.

Back in Dr. Reed's office...

"Mario, you've been sitting there for ten minutes without saying a word," Dr. Reed observes gently. "Where did you go?"

I blink, realizing I've been lost in that memory. "Church," I say simply.

"Tell me about that."

"I was five when I first gave my life to Christ. It was the most beautiful, accepted, loved feeling I'd ever experienced. The whole church celebrated me and Junior. My grandmother cried tears of joy. I thought I'd finally done something that would make Senior proud."

Dr. Reed leans forward. "But it didn't?"

"He was disgusted. Said I only did it to show off, that those people didn't care about me. That was the first time I realized that even God couldn't make me worthy in his eyes."

"And the Bible?"

My throat tightens. "Every time I tried to study Scripture after that, I ended up beaten. Senior would use the Bible as a weapon—if I messed up one word of my Easter speech, the rubber hose came out. I started to think God and pain were the same thing."

Dr. Reed was quiet for a long moment. "Mario, that wasn't God who hurt you. That was a man who used God's Word as a tool of abuse. There's a difference between the message and the messenger."

"But how do I separate them? Every time I hear Scripture, I feel that rubber hose. Every time I'm in church, I remember being five years old and so desperate for love that I'd give my heart to anyone who'd accept it."

"You were a little boy seeking what every child deserves—unconditional love and acceptance. The fact that you found it in God's House, even briefly, tells me your spirit knew where to look. The tragedy is that a man who should have reflected God's love chose to reflect something else entirely."

I nodded, feeling tears starting. "I miss that feeling, though. That moment when the whole church celebrated me. When I felt like I belonged somewhere."

"That feeling was real, Mario. That was God's Love. What happened afterward was Senior 's choice to corrupt that love, but it doesn't make the original feeling less real or less valid."

"So how do I get back to that five-year-old who walked down that aisle? How do I separate God from the people who hurt me in His Name?"

Dr. Reed smiles gently. "The same way you're learning to separate love from pain in your relationships. One revelation at a time. One choice at a time. One prayer at a time."

For the first time in years, I feel like maybe I could walk down that aisle again.

Not because I'm desperate for acceptance, but because I'm ready to accept myself.

Maybe God has been waiting for me to come home all along.

I got up to leave, and the otherwise dreary day gave way as the sun began to beam bright through the windows, engulfing me. It felt warm and familiar, like an embrace I'd been missing without even knowing it.

Dr. Reed looked over her glasses and smirked. "Look, it seems like God's love and light are already shining on you. Enjoy your day, Mario," she said, and returned back to her notepad.

I smiled, basking in the sunlight and God's love, feeling something I hadn't felt in years—the possibility that maybe I wasn't as alone as I thought. Maybe the God I met at five years old had been waiting patiently for me to find my way back home.

"*Chirp, chirp,*" the dark, feathered bird sang as it stood on my windowsill. I lay in my bed and squinted my eyes as the bright light from the sun beamed into my room through the orange, pleated curtains that draped my window. The wind wafted through the slightly ajar window and forced a bubble within the curtain, knocking over the picture frames that were placed on a nearby end table. I remember feeling the breeze and discerning this gentle wind from all the others this fall.

I awoke mid-sleep, rubbed my eyes, and stretched while letting out a loud and tacky yawn. I tossed the sheets which were covering me onto the ground and thought, *God, it's awfully warm in here.* But when my feet hit the floor, it reminded me that there was still a chill in the air. I walked to my closet and slipped into my house shoes, then walked to the window to draw the curtains back.

To my amazement, the once dreary, tedious morning was replaced by a lovely and spectacular new day. Once I opened the window, the bird that awoke me from my stolid and very restful sleep flew frantically away from the window. It perched itself on a branch that was near my home and began singing harmoniously again. The sights were so serene and breathtaking; I stood there in awe. When I finally closed my mouth before the fly that danced in the air flew into it, I smiled a smile that stretched from ear to ear.

I saw a circus of insects frolicking around. The ants appeared to have races on the ground, while the butterflies danced the salsa in the currents of wind. The bees chased after each other and the birds played sweet ballads in their choir for the flowers who swayed in the breeze. The buds of roses began to blossom, while the bumblebees stole their nectar prematurely.

All these sings signaled spring. Spring indicates change—change in season, change of weather, and change of life. It's the season for lovers, new and old. Only a poet can appreciate its immaculate beauty and transitional exquisiteness. Spring is the most beautiful season I have ever seen, and I take pleasure in it every year.

Perhaps I focus so intently on spring's beauty because there has been so much darkness planted in my life. The basement. The blood. The rubber hose. The family who left me wilting on floors while they flourished. The Unrequited Lover who kept me in shadows like some dirty little secret they were afraid to let bloom.

After years of being trampled down, after having my spirit pruned back to almost nothing, my soul craves beauty like a flower craves sunlight. I'm starving for something beautiful to grow from all this ugliness.

Spring represents the rebirth I desperately need to take root in my own life. If flowers can push through frozen ground, if trees can bloom again after winter tries to kill them, if nature can transform from dead-looking to gorgeous, then maybe I can too. Every bud that opens feels like proof that coming back to life is possible. Every bird song sounds like hope taking flight.

This is why I notice every detail of this morning, why I'm soaking up each breeze and blossom. I am a man learning to see beauty again after years of trauma. I am someone who needs to believe in fresh starts, in new growth, in the possibility that what seems dead can just be dormant—waiting for the right season to bloom again.

If spring can happen after winter's worst, then maybe I can flourish after a lifetime of being told I'll never amount to anything.

I became overjoyed at the splendor of the sights outside and rushed down the narrow hall to turn the heat off, even though the floor was still quite cool to the touch. *I won't be needing this for a while.* I continued to walk briskly down the hallway, stumbling over my slippers. I nearly fell to the ground and hit my head on the "falling ball" glass cocktail table I saw at Value City Furniture and had to have.

I arrived at the door and fumbled with the locks, and I remember several distinct profane words that popped into my head at this time, none of which helped me with the door. I stood on my porch as the songs of the birds echoed tranquility. I watched peacefully and observed everything. As I closed my eyes and sighed, I took in another deep breath to ingest the essence of spring, which plunged me into a placid self-comfort, interrupted only by the thoughts in my mind.

As seconds turned to minutes and minutes began to multiply themselves, the automatic alarm on my coffee maker signaled it was 8:14 in the morning and proceeded to process a pot of coffee. A dusty, clunky, older model Oldsmobile raced through the neighborhood and polluted the air with its thick, viscous cloud of fumes. I coughed and waved my arm to dissipate the cloud. After several minutes the fumes subsided, and a pleasant aroma of fresh Belgian Hazelnut Coffee saturated the air. I got a cup and returned to the porch to sit and watch and drink my coffee.

I find spring to be the most romantic and sensual of all the seasons. My admiration for the spring stems from my fondness for the many blossoms that flourish during spring: roses, orchids, and snapdragons are my plants of choice. In addition to the lovely flowers that thrive in spring, the warm and tepid temperatures make spring life even more favorable to me.

I admired the bountiful mass of flowers that cascaded through during spring, bringing with them their delightful fragrances. The way their perfume fills the air and intoxicates the neighborhood is my primary reason why I'm fond of spring. On the first couple of days of spring this year, I began to recognize the growth of flowers that occupies an area of my backyard. I peeked out the door, peering toward the flowers to confirm my previous assessment.

"They will be blossoming pretty soon," I said to Shon, Junior's fiancée, who had been staying with us.

"Not this soon. I haven't even seen any bees yet," Shon said while drying her hands.

She walked to the door to see what I was gazing at. She looked at me and gave me an, "I got better things to do than look at stupid plants" kind of look, turned her lips up, and walked into the kitchen to resume her previous task. I opened the door but didn't step out, and as I stuck my head out, a yellow jacket zoomed by my head and swarmed by the door. My natural reaction kicked in, and I jumped back and slammed the screen door shut. I started to point the wasp out to Shon, but it was early in the morning and I didn't want to start any confrontation today. However, I did examine the yard from my present position and smelled the sweet scent of spring in the air.

"Close that door. It ain't summer yet. I'm getting cold," Shon stated belligerently. I conceded and closed the door.

As days turned to a week, I returned to the backyard, but this time only to perform spring-cleaning chores. But to my surprise, the once young buds of flowers were now mature roses and orchids. My eyes protruded like a child's eyes on Christmas morning before examining their gifts. I proceeded over to inspect the flowers, pausing to check for any bees before I touched them. I didn't want any unexpected (or even expected) stings. I bent over to take a whiff of the plant's fragrance, ignoring the possible sinus attack I may have, and became elated and inebriated by its perfume.

At this point, I totally forgot about my chores in the yard and began to pick a couple of orchids and roses. I departed toward the house, nervously aware of the multitude of insects flying around. *One of them could be a bee,* I thought, rushing into the house. I love spring but hate the insects that thrive during spring. Once in the house, Shon let out a joyous holler.

"Those flowers look beautiful," she stated, bending over to smell them and looking up at me with a pleased smile. She took one in her hand and kept it positioned near her nose and danced slightly with it. When she noticed I was watching, she regained her composure, but she couldn't contain her excitement. I didn't feel embarrassed for her because I knew exactly how she felt. I placed them in a crystal vase on the kitchen table for display, so that every time I went into the kitchen I could see and smell these delightful specimens. Seeing them puts a smile on my face and reminds me of how beautiful Mother Nature really is.

I also love the warm spring sun as it beats down upon my face as I look toward the sky. Soothing, touching my skin like satin sheets, while the wind caresses my neck and takes me away, and brings me back ever slowly. "Oh, it's hot," I said while fanning myself with a folded piece of paper.

"You can say that again," my friend FaLessia said as she took another sip of her sweet tea.

Little did I know at that moment that this quiet, self-proclaimed introvert who preferred the shadows and rarely ventured out of her house would eventually become my wife. FaLessia, sitting there in the heat with her iced tea, was destined to be the woman who would help me rise from the ashes of my broken past. But this spring afternoon, she was simply my friend, my companion in the sweltering heat, unaware that our friendship was the seedling of something far more profound.

"The Heat" by Toni Braxton was on full blast on the radio. *What an appropriate song*, I thought. I refused to speak for fear that talking would increase the heat. Not saying I'm full of hot air, of course. Even the dogs in the backyard gave in to the heat. Cleopatra was laid out in the yard with her tongue dangling out, while Midnight retreated to her house. The children in our neighborhood played as if there was no heat wave at the beginning of spring.

"Mario, wasn't it snowing a couple of days ago? That's Michigan for you, snow today and heatwave tomorrow. I wish it could make up its mind what it plans to do," FaLessia stated as I nodded my head in agreement. Yet, I appreciate the warmth as a refreshing shift in the climate. I enjoyed the chilling cold temperatures in winter, but I'm even happier it's gone—for now. Kids of every age lit up with excitement when they heard the ice cream man coming. They hurried to the curb, eagerly gathering around his truck just like bees drawn to honey. The neighborhood was filled with sounds of laughter and arguing as children gathered under the shade trees that lined the streets. The radio announcer interrupted the song for a special announcement.

"It's a scorcher out there! If you're outside, make sure you have sunscreen and drink plenty of fluids. If you're not in the shade, or under an air conditioner, I can't see how you're managing the heat. Here's a new one by the late Aaliyah called 'Rock the Boat.' Maybe this will help you cool off."

The song played on the radio as we rocked to the beats of the song. I grabbed my glass to sip my iced tea, but the ice had melted and made it bitter and watery. Everything this day was still; all the creatures either migrated to cool places or were too hot to move. Even the clouds in the sky were still, providing little to no shade. FaLessia tried to get up out of her seat, but the sweat from her body made her muggy and the perspiration stained her outfit. I poured my watered-down tea on the ground and within seconds it was absorbed. The crackling of the sun and jets flying were the only activity in the sky. I sat wondering what happened to the birds. As the sun repositioned itself overhead, we also had to relocate to the shade. We sat the remainder of the day in the shade, enjoying the warm breezes of heat as it descended from the clouds, gently cooling us.

Springtime is the season where all creatures and plants come alive. The rays of the bright and immense sun reanimate the living to blossom again. The most enjoyable and pleasing time is when efflorescence ends and the spring blossoms unfold. Countless flowers sway in the wind with a rhythmical fashion, as to a beat spraying the air with intoxicating fragrances, which are delightful as well as unforgettable. Fragrances reminiscent of floral shops accompanied the mild and pleasant temperatures that are associated with spring weather. All this and more make spring weather the most enjoyable weather I have ever felt, and I wouldn't trade spring for any other season.

I wonder what Dr. Reed would make of how I'm experiencing today. It's been a couple weeks since my last session with her. After those intense memories we unearthed—the basement, the blood-stained walls, the rubber hose—I needed some distance. I've made excuses as to why I couldn't keep my appointments with her, but the truth is I needed some alone time, some space to let those revelations settle without having to dig up more buried trauma.

In the aftermath of losing my job—the Unrequited Lover's final act of retaliation—I spent days in a fog of anger and hurt. But something Dr. Reed said kept echoing in my mind: "Stop trying to resurrect what God has already buried." Maybe getting fired was God closing a door I kept trying to force open.

I landed a new job at the Flint Public Library, which feels like a fresh start. The quiet environment, surrounded by books and stories of transformation, seems fitting for this season of my life. Things are looking OK. Better than OK, actually. The library is where I met FaLessia. But I still keep a measure of hope in my heart for the Unrequited Lover. Against my better judgment and the judgment of Dr. Reed, we kept in contact. Their life moved on and so did mine, but for some reason, we keep meeting.

Sorrow began to fill my heart. With great force I hold back the tears as I evaluate everything that's happening. If this was another time, another season, would me and the Unrequited Lover have a future? Or will we be left with fragmented memories of a shattered and twisted past?

FaLessia left to go home, and I'm kind of glad that she did, because at this moment I needed to self-reflect. I started writing more. I've always written, even as a little kid. I remember my mother's friend Cali read one of my works when I was about ten and said that I would one day be a writer. 20 years later, she passed away; like my mother, she was also a victim of domestic violence. In fact, this is how she and Mama met. Normally, these two women would never encounter each other: Cali was a vibrant, middle-aged white woman, and mama at this moment was an hourly employee living off of food stamps. But somehow, their paths crossed. I would like to take this moment to thank Cali for having the foresight, or prophetic gift, of looking into my life and who I was at that time and see that I would be an author. And as I sit here today writing this, I do this with the memory of Cali.

I always kept my journal near me: A blue book that had water drops on it, titled "Meditation Journal." It was a blank book that allowed me to write my thoughts and poems in it. As I sit here, one pops up.

Passing

Two moments in time.
    Always passing.
Almost meeting.
Yet passing.
Passively flirting.
Jesting at times, yet passing.
    Two celestial bodies
coasting through space.
Ultimately set upon a collision course.
Destined to collide.
Resulting in an orgasmic astronomical explosion.
Scattering ourselves throughout the universe.
Yet we passed.
Almost.
But yet passing.
Not gracing.
Never touching, always passing.
    Two seasons yearning to meet.
Ethereally, you bloom bright
In the spring sun.
I, rising to meet you,
found you withered away
As the summer winds blew upon you.
Two seasons missed.

Almost meeting yet passing.
Blooming, flowers, growing alternatively,
seasonally.
Yet passing.
     Two spirits creeping out at night.
Angelically floating through the crystal air.
Reaching yearning to touch.
Invisible lovers.
Seers of the world blinded to each other.
Two invisible spirits seeking to touch.
Almost meeting.
Yet passing.
Blind entities reaching to touch,
invisible only to each other.
Yet passing.
     Passing.
Always passing.
Never meeting.
Always eager.
Always passing.
Destined to meet.
Yet we keep on.
Passing.

Tears flow like rivers down my cheek. I know that the supposed love I have for this person is as forbidden as it is impossible. Toxic. Deliberate. But damn if it didn't feel good. I wanted to hear the voice again. I'm looking for crumbs when I should be feasting at the table. I know I'm going to have to tell Dr. Reed what I did, but sometimes I can't but help myself to the vicious cycle of climatic exchanges knowing the inevitable result would be having my heart and psyche crushed. Sometimes even feeling something is better than feeling nothing. I began to look at this pattern and realized that the numbing of my heart was abated by finding and looking for love and expressions of love that will inevitably fill some form of void that existed.

At this point, to my satisfaction, if you will—pardon me if I laugh and turn on with extreme sublime smugness—the wedding didn't go happen. The Unrequited Lover was no longer engaged.

Give me a minute while I mourn this breakup…moment's over.

I dialed the Unrequited Lover's phone number. Each ring echoes louder and louder in my ear and with each ring I sit there holding my breath, waiting for the sound of my lover.

"Hello." Very dry.

"Hey, how are you doing today?" I ask, playing coy. I cared somewhat, but mainly just wanted to hear their voice.

"I'm doing OK." This response was both minimalistic and dismissive. *So we're going to play this cat and mouse game? OK, game on.*

"Well, I'm doing well. Thanks for asking," I shot back.

No response. I've been down this road many times. The games we play. The witty repartee we exchange. *This is so us,* I say while I sit on the line in silence. I wasn't gonna be the one to break this time. *You want me as much as I want you, and I know it,* I think, manifesting in myself this relationship, this nothingness.

After what felt like hours, the silence was broken. "What are you doing?"

Checkmate. "Sitting here thinking of you," I responded back with a snare of a tiger in the delivery of a deer.

"Well, those are good thoughts," the Unrequited Lover responded.

"Sometimes," I counter back. *Gosh, Mario, you can be a little stinker sometimes.*

"Well, if that's the case, then why even call?"

No, they didn't, I thought. However, that question really resonated with me. *Why am I calling? Why play this little game? The result is not going to change. We're never going to be together. The Unrequited Lover is never going to provide me what I want, never going to be what I need, who I need. Why do I keep putting myself into situations where I know the result will be hurt?* In this situation, the person causing me pain is some-one I wish would not hurt me. This level of introspective examination is taking a proverbial knife to surgically alter this situation I put myself in. I know how this ends, but I keep putting myself in the exact same situation. Someone once said that insanity is doing the same thing over and over again and expecting a different result. I'm either a damn fool or crazy. Hell, I might even be both.

"Well," the Unrequited Lover asked.

"Well, I don't know why," I responded back, still deep in my thoughts. This feels so different than how I've interacted before. I don't want to be on this phone call.

"Well, if you don't know, then maybe you shouldn't have called."

Suddenly, I hung up the phone. I felt empowered. I felt a surge of "take that," if you will, in my spirit. I remember pre-cell phone days. The ability to hang up with a physical phone and slam it down gave a visceral feel of your frustration, as opposed to the new age of a cell phone where you just hit end. But this feeling was short-lived. The phone rang, and although I did not have caller ID, I knew who was on the other end.

"Really?" the Unrequited Lover asked.

"Yes, really," I responded. "You really frustrated me."

We spar back and forth for a few minutes. Out of all the things I could say to or about the Unrequited Lover, not many people could proverbially spar with me, or put me in my place. They had this down to a science, and I loved that.

After our spar, a moment of silence drifted over the phone, hanging like clouds in the sky, hanging like clothes on a clothing line on a warm summer's day, floating and hanging like lilies in the wind. But then there was a break.

"If you hang up on me again, I will never talk to you again," the Un-requited Lover directed.

Oh really? My face frowned up as if I had drunk a glass of sour milk. Nausea and upset filled my stomach equally, and the only thing I felt like doing at that moment was responding as I did.

"Do you promise?"

The Unrequited Lover replied, "Yes."

I hung up.

No tears streamed down my face. No heartache was felt. I was truly numb. I sat by the phone for a few minutes, half hoping to receive a phone call back, half hoping I did not. There was a finality to this conversation, one that was so foreign to me. I knew this would be the last time we had a phone conversation. To this day, we have never spoken again. It's time to take it to my book.

Dear Seeker

When you come for me,
your prize wages
of an ancient war.
I lie broken.
Stolid hollow pieces.
   Pieces of a monument
long ago ruined
like the ancient Egyptians.
Time has been cruel.
   Defeated, come my Dear Seeker
Claim your prize,
O valiant Deceiver.
You blinded me with your lies.
You stole what I would have offered to you.
An altar in my heart I created for you.
   I've grown weary over the years.
My race has been run.
I escaped the prison of your mind.
   I hid on Jupiter,
but you created the rings to bind me.
I pleaded to escape to Pluto.
You sent the cold to freeze me.
   Mercury then became my home,
but your anger burned

and scorched me,
much like the sun.
I was consumed by the fire.
    I rested on Earth,
and life has kissed me.
But now you exist here,
my seeker.
    Your love is poison to my lips.
Your existence confounds me.
I have no more fight.
    When you open the door
into your habitation,
beaming resolved that you win.
Know that I have escaped you again.
    Dear Seeker.

.

As I close my journal, I also close the chapter on the Unrequited Lover. Our season has passed. The moment is over. The final curtain has been called, and the orchestra exits. Wherever you are, I do not pay you homage—I pay you dust. Wonder what Dr. Reed would think of this.

Yet in this ending, I sense a beginning. Spring has taught me about rebirth, about the cycles of life and love. And perhaps, in the quiet presence of FaLessia, in her gentle strength and patient soul, lies the seed of a love that won't pass by, but will instead take root and flourish in the seasons to come.

There's something almost sacred about this symmetry—how God sends both spring and FaLessia at the exact moment I'm learning to believe in beauty again. Her grace mirrors the gentle way flowers unfold after winter's harshness. Her patient quietness reflects the way trees wait through seasons of dormancy before they bloom. Where the Unrequited Lover demanded I remain hidden in shadows, FaLessia simply exists in the light, comfortable with who she is, teaching me by example that love doesn't have to hurt to be real.

Maybe this is how God works—not through dramatic interventions, but through the quiet miracle of right people arriving in the right seasons. FaLessia doesn't know she's part of my resurrection story, just as spring doesn't know it's saving my soul. But here they both are, proof that what seems dead can come back to life, that what's been buried can bloom again.

The phoenix prepares to rise, and though I don't yet know it, my future wife sits beside me, sharing iced tea and weathering the storm of this Michigan heat. Sometimes deliverance looks like seasons changing. Sometimes it looks like a quiet woman with gentle strength, arriving when you're ready to stop accepting shadows and start believing in sunlight.

Chapter 9: Broken Early

Life is truly taking form for me right now. Although there have been ups and downs—or as Yolanda Adams says, "Mountain high, valley low"—I've been embracing this newness I feel within myself. However, there still is a duality that exists within my life. Inescapable and purposefully unreachable, yet it exists.

I sit here in Dr. Reed's office, and we recap my last several weeks. As usual, Dr. Reed sits astute, the consummate professional, taking notes, judgment vacant on her face, and ushering in with her a presence of peace and ease. Unmistakably, those virtues are disarming and allow me to release whatever I have inside of me.

However, as the floodgates of memories arise and pour out, there are some rivers that dare not be bathed in. Some outpours that the dam's walls must contain. Some secrets, some boxes, some memories are too earth-shattering, too detrimental, too vulnerable for any setting outside of the Throne of God. No earthly ears should ever hear them.

I feel all my mechanisms, all the years of walls and barriers that are placed up high, and I can't help but notice a slight breach. Dr. Reed sits and takes immaculate notes. I can't help but wonder again what she is writing, and if I could peer into those notes to see what she's writing so intently, so deliberately.

As she's writing, I walk over to the window. As I gaze out, I compare who I am to what's going on outside. As raindrops dance down the windowsill, I can't help but think that even the sky is crying, much like how I feel on the inside.

Much of the recounting I've done with Dr. Reed has been centered around my spiritual growth and indiscriminate sexual encounters. Remember, I said there's a duality to me. I've been going to church with Mama quite frequently on Friday nights and have started going occasionally on Sunday mornings—if I didn't stay out too late.

Now it's not that I had these encounters out of some barbaric need. Afterward, I felt rather disgusted. I regretted it. But for some reason, I still went and did it. Like a cat that hunts flies in the house, who stares out the window wanting to be outside. Although this cat is domesticated and staying indoors protects it from obvious dangers outside, it still longs to venture outdoors and hunt. Deep within its DNA, the urge to explore and hunt remains strong because that's its natural instinct.

It's a ritual, if you will call it that. I would occasionally have hookups. Sometimes no names, random, faultless. Always protected, though. Indiscriminate and pitiful. These encounters felt like taking control—choosing to give my body instead of having it taken, even if the aftermath left me hollower than before. I would go home sometimes and take long baths and scrub myself off the stench. Maybe if I go to church and put extra in the collection plate, God will forgive me even more. Or get up in line at church and ask for prayer, and then maybe the ministers or pastors can pray this away.

As I watch the rain fall on the deserted parking lot, I sense the emptiness in my heart. Despite moments of relief, nothing ever truly satisfies me. The loss of little Mario is something I will always grieve.

Many times, people have told me to get over it, to stop living in the past. Sometimes, it's hard because the past has deeply affected—or even destroyed—a part of me. I don't think I could ever truly be whole again. I don't think I could ever truly give myself 100% to anyone. I have learned in life to always hold something back. Yes, you may get 80%, but 20% I'm keeping to myself. These inescapable feelings and memories force me to hide a part of myself because I've been made to believe like part of me is so unlovable, so ugly, so unattractive, so unwanted, so devious that even the people who bore me did not love me. Even through familial ties, they couldn't love me.

So it must be me.

To be loved, I must hide a part of me. Because if people truly see me, maybe they will see what others saw, that they all hated, that they beat, that they ignored. That part of me that will push everyone away. There is a part of me that is that unlovable, unlikable, intolerable.

I can't help but believe that it is like I was born with a stain on me. We hear about the scarlet letter, but I often think I have a marking on me that other people see and want no part of. As Langston Hughes would say, I'll wear a mask. Never let anyone get too close, never too deep. As I said, everyone will leave me.

I cry.

Dr. Reed again breaches protocol and quietly walks over to the window with her back against the wall, watching with me.

"Mario, I've always loved the rain also," she says in her natural, soothing voice. "Many people look at it with sadness, but I look at it differently. The rain serves so many purposes. One purpose is to water, to give life and sustenance to the world. Many things are dying, drying out, yearning for something to quench their thirst. Like the valley of dry bones in the Bible. I look at these as blessings falling down upon us and giving us new life, feeding us and enriching us.

"And the second part is the rain comes to wash away—wash away the stench from yesterday, the dirt from life, taking away the old and making room for the new. And after the rain, God puts His bow in the sky, and everything that went away when the clouds were there, when the rains prevailed, came out from hiding. A newness comes about. You ever watch and hear how the birds start chirping? All the insects come out? It's almost like a joyous occasion after the rain.

"Like our tears, the raindrops are like a cleansing of our soul. They cascade down our faces to wash away pain and cleanse our bodies, our souls, of the hurt that human life has caused us. That's why I've always been a proponent of telling people not to hold in tears—let them out. It is a release."

She hands me a tissue and pats me on my back. "Go ahead and let it out, Mario. Remember that you may bend, but you will never be broken."

I quickly turn to her and blurt out, "Oh really? I was broken early."

Like a child who spoke out a secret, I cover my mouth and cry harder. She guides me to the couch.

"I see. We were wrapping, but I think we need to have more conversation. What is this 'broken early' that you speak of?"

I sit there shaking my head vehemently. The tears that streamed down my face poured out like the water from Heaven when Noah was in the ark. I shake, and Dr. Reed sits, watches, and never says a word.

For a moment, I regret being here. I regret that I blurted that out. For a brief moment, I hate that Dr. Reed sees this part of me. I hate that she doesn't comfort me. I hate how performative I'm being.

I lived it over 15 years ago, but some hurts and some wounds never heal. I know people say time heals all wounds, but sometimes I feel like that's not true. There's no healing that will go forth. It may be insufferable to think of that, but sometimes we learn to deal with the pain. Or after so long, the pain becomes numb. We become so used to the pain that we can pull it close like a pillow at night. It can be so tangible that we can touch it.

Compartmentalization is a thing, and sometimes we place things out of our mind, out of our way. But I believe it will always be there. No matter what we try—prayer, therapy, pills, alcohol, or sex—nothing will fix it.

Just like Paul wrote to the Corinthians when he went before the Lord three times asking God for deliverance from a physical ailment, God told him, "My grace is sufficient for thee." Not all pain and discomfort will go away. I learned that in church when Pastor was preaching about how becoming a Christian doesn't mean that everything is going to be perfect after you become saved. That being a Christian means you're going to endure many things, because our Savior endured many things. And what more are we if our Savior had to endure these things? For He said that because of me you will endure many things. The world hated Him first.

Through tear-filled eyes, I catch a glimpse of Dr. Reed—hands clasped, sitting with extreme posture. I lock eyes with her, and a sense of consolation takes over me. I realize that even if she did try to comfort me, I at this point do not want human touch.

She looks at me with what I can discern as either pity, sadness, or concern and says, "You can't keep letting this control you. You've kept this secret too long. Speak it out."

Her voice shifts between professionalism and pastoring. Her words are no longer requests, but a directive. Something shifts in her demeanor. The gentle therapist disappears, replaced by a woman who's done battle with demons before.

"Speak it out," she says more forcefully.

The tears stop. I become afraid.

"Speak it out," she says as she points toward me.

I sit up. My defenses are activated. I scan around looking for a place to retreat but find no home. She continues pointing her finger at me and says with the voice and flare of lightning, "SPEAK IT OUT."

And suddenly I'm seven years old again, the words pouring out like blood from a reopened wound.

Memory: Innocence Lost

They were nice kids. We would always get together with my cousins over at my granny's house on the north side of Flint. It was the official hangout of so many people in our family. The house wasn't very big, so we would always be cramped together into spaces. We had so many different family members coming in and out of the house, staying some nights.

This night was hot. As usual with poverty-ridden families such as mine, no one had air conditioning, and we had only one fan. This is the problem when you stay with people who are accustomed to the southern heat. That night, everybody was sprawled throughout the house. It wasn't a time for us all to be crammed together in one room.

I remember lying in bed, tossing and turning as the heat was almost unbearable. The windows in Granny's house never opened. I slept in the room by the front door. I liked this room because it would always catch the breeze throughout the house. We had the doors open, so when the breeze came, for some reason it circled in this room.

Granny's house was interesting. It was not musty but had a particular scent. Granny would always be frying chicken and making greens or some other type of southern food, and it was like the walls absorbed that scent. Normally it was not a problem, but at night in the heat, the smell was too much.

I tossed and turned, and then I heard the door creak open. A family member came in, gestured for silence by placing a finger to their lips, and quietly shut the door. This wasn't unusual—it was something we'd often experience. Sharing beds and personal space was typical for us, so it wasn't a major concern.

They got into bed with me. It was hot—real hot. We exchanged a few words because I couldn't get any sleep. I was a rather impressionable kid—strong-willed, but also impressionable, if that makes sense.

The next few moments shook my seven-year-old mind.

I was never taught the dangers of strangers, but this person wasn't a stranger. I was never taught that some touches were not okay. But as I lay in this bed, this person's hands surveyed my body, each request a command.

They left after a few minutes, and I laid there, confused at what happened. *What was the purpose of their hands? Their lips? Why was I supposed to do some of the things that they commanded me to do to them?*

This was the first time that sickness I felt in my stomach arose.

The door creaked again. They enter and carefully close the door behind them again. They take their clothes off. They get into the bed with me and resume the touching and lip play. I acquiesce and do as I am instructed to do.

And then there was a break. A tear, if you will.

Some details are not meant to be shared. Some memories not meant to be told. Some scabs are not meant to be removed.

What happened was innocence lost. Innocence stolen.

That hot night was the first night on which I was able to see demons. That summer night on the north side of Flint, little Mario, like Adam and Eve in the garden, was able to see good and evil.

The break, the breach, the tear was not only physical, but mental and spiritual. The human body is capable of enduring so much stress, so much pain, and can rebuild itself. But the human psyche? Not so much.

From that night forward, I never looked at an adult the same way. Or any person. The bond of family shifted. Trust in humanity shifted. The body is so giving, and sometimes it gives at the expense of who we truly are as a person. My body gave because it could. My heart broke because it could. And my spirit was broken because they did. I never felt safe enough to tell anybody. Lord knows I would have years of being around this person.

This is where I feel the marking occurred. From that day forward, I always felt seen—but not by the people I wanted to be seen by. Prior to this, nothing like this had ever happened. But after, it was as if a stench or a stain or marking was on me where all predators like this person knew. No words were ever exchanged. It was always a look, a gaze, something telling in their eyes that said, *"Hey, I know you. And I know what I can do to you."* As if they could smell the vulnerability, the broken places that made me an easy target. Once you've been prey, other predators know.

This is why I never liked to leave the house. Because every time I looked around, I would see these demons. I'd catch their gaze and even sometimes their touch when they thought no one was looking.

I've been marked.

And even after that, someone else saw the mark, the stain, and replaced the previous predator with themselves. They even made a makeshift bed in the garage of an abandoned building adjacent to my grandmother's house. And when my mother took us over there, I would always want to stay in the house. I didn't want to go outside and play because on that block, I knew that person was there. I knew what they would want to do.

But I had to go outside. Most of the time, other cousins didn't want to play with me, so I would always be left alone. It was an uncomfortable and familiar feeling.

I would see them walking down the street or peering through the curtains. In an almost rehearsed fashion, they would come around and joke with the family and then tell me to come with them.

I remember one time, I looked at my mother, watery-eyed, my eyes pleading, but were met with alcohol-induced eyes. They bore no resemblance to the woman I knew and offered no assistance. And so, I acquiesced.

To the garage. Onto the mildew-stained mattress with springs that poked out. Where I would be crying and you know the rest.

This happened countless times. In each instance, I felt a piece of me die away.

These spirits I attracted would be at get-togethers at our house. It was unimaginable to me that no one even asked. They knew who I was. They saw me for what they needed. They took it each time they needed it. I got to a point where I didn't fight anymore. It became the new norm.

I slide off the couch to the floor and curl into a ball and cry.

One of the things I used to do growing up, and even still to this day, is to make myself a bubble with my sheet. Many people never understood why. It served multiple reasons, but primarily, it was my cocoon. It was my shield from the outside world. Inside my bubble, there was only me. No threats, no hurt, no pain. I couldn't see outside. I would only see what was in my bubble or what my imagination could conjure up.

Often—remember I told you I can see demons?—I would see them floating around in my room. And the only consolation I had would be to put my sheet over my head and turn the fan on high to create a bubble. In that bubble, my cocoon, I found solace. Inside my cocoon, vultures wouldn't come up and use my body. The rubber hose had no place. No one could punch me.

I needed my cocoon at this time.

Dr. Reed lifted me up from the floor and sat me back on the couch.

"This was hard for you. I know, but it was necessary. You needed to confront and bring out those memories. Your silence has given them a shield, but your words have power, and you need to speak it out. Release that shame and that hurt and walk within the love that God has for you.

"Remember in the Bible it says that if the thief be found, he must restore sevenfold. We know who the thief is. He's been a deceiver from the beginning. That devil, those demons—they stole your youth. They stole your innocence. Don't let them steal your peace. God wants restoration to go forth in your life. I want that restoration for you."

She lifts my face to hers. "Do you want restoration?"

I don't say a mumbling word, but my eyes locked with hers say everything that needed to be said.

"Now I know that you can't go to them anymore. I wouldn't recommend it. And I'm not saying for you to go and tell everybody in your family what happened to you. But you must confront these things and build a wall of defense and go to God and allow Him to restore back to you what they stole, to give you a new life. Remember, the Bible tells us that we become a new creature in Christ, that old things are done away, that He's looking to do a new thing. Let Him do that new thing in your life right now, Mario."

Again, no words. Just tears. Just broken.

I sit there wondering: *How am I going to put myself together when I am shattered into so many pieces? How can I ever love someone or even have somebody love me when I am but a fractured, shadowed, and shattered version of what I should be?*

Dr. Reed gets up and retrieves a bowl from her bookshelf. She places it in my hand and says, "Look at this."

I hold it and it is heavier than I thought. It is a blue bowl with dusty orange, brown, and veins of yellow going through the bowl.

"Okay. It's a bowl. It looks nice." I'm wondering if we're going to go through some cleansing ceremony and we'll be using this bowl for it.

She says, "Mario, do you know what this is?"

I look at her.

"This bowl was used and fabricated by using a Japanese technique called Kintsugi."

I give her a strange look. She gives me a smile and says, "This technique is an art. They take broken pottery and mend it back together by utilizing gold. See, Mario, what was once originally a mediocre, inexpensive bowl that was broken and shattered to pieces is now an expensive piece of art because those broken pieces were put back together, improved from the original, and held together with gold.

"See, when it was broken, it was useless. But they figured out a way of taking what was perceived to be useless and turn it into something that has substantial value.

"I want you to sit with that. Don't let anyone look at you and think that because you are broken or were broken you are useless and have no value. God can take the broken pieces of you and mend them and put them back together so that they would be even more valuable than what was originally there. What we see as a mess, God can turn to a message. He can turn your test into a testimony.

"The Bible tells us in Psalm 51:17 that 'the sacrifices of God are a broken spirit: a broken and contrite heart, O God, thou wilt not despise.'"

She stands up and extends her arm. "I want you to take the first steps today. Step out of the darkness into the light. No more broken, but whole. No more loving in shadows. Yes, you were broken early, but it's not how we begin but how we end. Even God says the first shall be last and the last shall be first. Will you take those steps?"

Something in her words penetrates the fog of my shame. I don't have to carry this alone anymore. Maybe being broken isn't the end of my story. I rise, legs wobbling, not sure I have the strength to continue, but knowing I can't stay curled on this floor forever. I take her hand.

And I feel purposeful.

Chapter 10: The Deep Calls to Deep

I must be honest. It's been very difficult these last couple of sessions with Dr. Reed. The enormous number of doors and walls that have been torn down, revealing the unadulterated, grim nature of my past, has left me shaken on many fronts. But I can also say that with great resolve, I have found solace and comfort in knowing that my past is not a precursor to my future. That no matter what I've experienced in the past, what lies before me is bigger and better than what's in my past.

I'm not sure who told me this before, but they told me that we need to not focus on the past. This is why in a car your windshield is bigger than your rearview mirror. You are supposed to be able to look forward with greater view, but keeping a peripheral look on what is behind you.

Over the last several months, I have been going to church a lot more. There is something about this church, the ministers, that resonates with me. And although some churches do not believe that women should preach, the pastor being a woman in this instance doesn't affect me at all. I have learned throughout my studies that God has used many different people and objects to give forth His message. If God can speak through a donkey, a burning bush, and lightning, clearly He could use a woman.

Technically, if you look at who a minister is, it's someone who preaches the good news about Jesus Christ. And when you think about it, when Jesus died on the cross and rose, one of the first people He met was Mary. And after presenting Himself to Mary, she went off to tell everyone about who Jesus was. Arguably, she can be considered the first minister.

Outside of my newfound bond with the church, I started school also. I consider it odd for me to be able to go to school. I've never envisioned myself having a life. So many people talk about how they grew up wanting to be this or wanting to be that. I never had that. There was a rare time in which I wanted to become a forensic pathologist—very strange, but I did. But through all the things that have happened to me in my life, I literally stopped thinking about a future.

The words that echoed in my mind were something that Senior told me a long time ago: that I would never grow up to be anything. He said it to me for an extended period of time. And then when life started happening—with the fire that destroyed our home, the homelessness, the beatings, the rejection from family, the sexual abuse—I didn't envision any good thing that life could ever do for me.

All I'd learned and known was hurt and pain. Life became synonymous with loss, pain, and hurt. To envision more of this was simply not something I wanted to do. Through the normal course of human activity, I don't think any rational human who experienced what I've experienced would have wanted more of it. Envisioning a future gleaming with happiness and prosperity was so foreign to me, like water to a vagabond in the desert.

But nevertheless, I started a new job at a tech company, and in doing so, I had the opportunity to start an associate's degree in network administration. This was an opportunity that I would have never envisioned for myself, but it gave me purpose—something that I haven't felt in many, many years.

Purpose. The word itself, void of any true meaning, intangible like air. What was purpose? Even at 22, the idea of a purpose-filled life evaded me still. I strain to understand or even envision what contribution I could possibly have to life, to this world. The words of a song echoed in my mind: "Is my living in vain?" But I had to resolve that God has truly opened this door for me.

It's funny to think that way and feel that way as I lay here on a mattress in an empty three-bedroom home. Mama found love again and decided to move away. At that time, Junior, his baby mama, and their two children lived with us, as well as a family friend and her daughter. Mama announced that she was leaving and gave us thirty-day notice—which amounted to no notice.

I was going to move out a while ago, but she'd talked me into staying so that I could help financially contribute to the household. I ended up giving up my apartment. So, when she sprung this news on me, it was very disconcerting.

Everyone quickly had to shuffle around their resources to get themselves a home. And within a few days, everyone except me found a place. I was able to get a new apartment back at Arena East, but there was a three-week delay. Everyone packed up all their things and moved out, taking everything with them.

I remember coming home from work and helping everyone move out and get settled into their own new homes. I was genuinely happy for everyone. Once everyone got completely moved out, I remember looking around the house and realizing I had nothing left but this mattress and a few items I had for my new apartment.

They took all the silverware, glasses, plates, almost all the canned foods except the few that they didn't want. Hell, they even took the baking soda that was used to refresh the refrigerator. And when they left, for two weeks, *no one* came and checked on me.

Everybody leaves me.

I would get off work, close up the curtains, and sit on my mattress. At least I still had electricity. I would throw on some old VHS movies and sit in the dark watching TV and eating whatever I could scrape up. The landlord was trying to take possession of the property, but I needed more time, so I had to squat in the house, avoiding whenever he would show up, turning down the TV if he ever popped up.

There was one time that one of my friends, Tiffany, dropped me off from work. She needed to use the restroom, and I tried to stop her from coming in, but she insisted. When she looked around the house and saw no tables, no furniture— a couple of boxes, a mattress, small-screen TV and VCR on a milk crate—the look of panic and sadness shrouded her face like a silk veil.

She inquired what was going on, and I told her the whole story. But the hope was that within a week and a half, I would move into my own apartment. I just had to tough it out for a few more days.

Tiffany sighed, and I was relieved she hugged me and left. Although this type of situation was customary for me, I knew that some people would find it objectionable. There were many times in which we didn't have water, and at the Flint Public Library, I would sneak upstairs to the men's bathroom in the executive wing to wash up in that bathroom.

I remember how angry FaLessia got when she discovered that we didn't have running water and then our electricity got cut off. I never quite understood her rage. *Everybody gets stuff cut off, right?* It wasn't my fault. But her background afforded her the luxury, from my viewpoint, to not experience these kinds of hardships in life, which for me were very common. We didn't go a season without one of the essentials being cut off.

Later, I hear a knock at the door, and fear grips me again. It wasn't fear that someone would come in and hurt me. At this age, I made the determination that nothing else that lived and walked on this earth would ever hurt me again—and I was willing to die to ensure that. My greatest fear was that the landlord would arrive, leaving me homeless with absolutely nowhere to go. *Been there, done that.*

I peer out through a crack in the curtains and see my friend and coworker Tiffany with a box. *What is she doing here?*

I rush to the door and open it, and there she stands, grinning from ear to ear with a box full of food. She looks me in my face and says, "Now, I know you're going to not accept this, but I don't want to hear it. I'm giving this to you now. I love you. Take it, eat, and get some rest."

She pushes the box into my arms, flicks her hair, gets to her car, and drives off. And I stood there at the door, almost in tears, because this kind of human experience was uncommon for me.

You would think the hardships that I endured were because I didn't have any family. Quite the contrary. At that very house, I had family right down the road, about five houses down. My grandparents owned property all throughout Flint. At that time, Senior was less than a mile from my home. I had quite a bit of family in the city. But what I didn't have was love and support. The idea of family helping each other out was not something I was familiar with.

Even my immediate family were so involved in their new lives and their new houses that they moved into that I was not even an echo, a blip on their radar.

I've learned a long time ago that life is scary. At 22, I would say that a third of my life was spent alone, unprotected, navigating this world solo. And so, I live my life like that—never relying on anyone but myself, always side-eyeing when someone seems nice. The perpetual thought of, "What do you want?" always echoes in my mind. The constant fear that if I let you get close, you're going to hurt me. Looking over my shoulder, questioning everyone and everything. This was not life.

Lying here in the darkness—sweet, cold, calculated darkness—I ironically find peace.

I love the darkness. It provides a covering for my despair, a cloak to shroud me from life. The darkness became my peace. But inside the darkness lived its own demons.

From a young age, I was able to see spirits. In the deep quiet of night, glowing beams would reveal once-invisible figures, swirling through the air. Though I watched them, fear kept me from trying to interact. Eventually, I reasoned that maybe my imagination was responsible for what I saw. Still, whenever darkness fell, I sensed an unseen audience watching as these shapes appeared and danced before me.

Tonight, as I lay on my mattress staring at the ceiling, the familiar stirring begins. The air grows thick, electric with unseen presence. In my peripheral vision, shadows begin to move independently of any light source. They drift across the walls like smoke given form, some tall and elongated, others small and skittering.

One figure materializes more clearly than the others—a tall, dark silhouette standing in the corner of the room. Its outline wavers like heat rising from summer pavement, but its eyes are fixed on me with an intensity that makes my skin crawl. I can feel its gaze like ice water in my veins.

"I see you," I whisper into the darkness, my voice barely audible.

The figure tilts its head, as if acknowledging my words. Other shadows begin to gather, drawn by our interaction. They circle the edges of the room like wolves surrounding prey, their movements fluid and predatory.

There were a few times in my life I could remember being scared because something I saw in the darkness tried to attack me. Trust me, I'm not crazy, but literally, it was like a ghost who saw me looking at him and attacked me. Tonight feels different, though. More charged. More dangerous.

The tall figure steps forward, separating itself from the corner. As it moves, the temperature in the room seems to drop. My breath becomes visible in small puffs. The other shadows grow bolder, creeping closer to my mattress.

I sit up, my heart pounding. "What do you want?" I ask, though I'm not sure I want an answer.

The figure raises what might be its arm, pointing directly at me. Its mouth opens—a dark void within darkness—and though no sound emerges, I hear words in my mind: *You belong with us. In the darkness. Stop fighting it.*

The other shadows begin to whisper, their voices overlapping in a chorus of temptation: *"Give up. Let go. Stop trying to find the light. This is where you belong. This is what you are."*

I feel a pulling sensation, as if invisible hands are trying to drag me deeper into something I can't see. The darkness around me pulses like a living thing, breathing, waiting.

"No," I say, my voice stronger now. "I don't belong to you."

But even as I say the words, I feel the familiar doubt creeping in. Maybe they're right. Maybe this darkness is all I'll ever know. Maybe this emptiness, this isolation, this spiritual wasteland is my true home.

The figures press closer. I can feel their presence like cold fingers on my skin. The darkness whispers promises of peace, of ending the struggle, of finally belonging somewhere.

As I peer out into the darkness, I always refrain from speaking or touching anything. I heard a Scripture in church once that said the deep calls to the deep. If I reach out and touch the darkness, will something touch me back? If I call out, will something hear me and answer?

It was as if there was no escape from the tortures of normal life and the constant fear of hurt and angst, or the primordial fear of the darkness which I've become so acquainted with. I truly feel a pulling to come to one side or the other.

"Deep calls to deep," I whisper, remembering the Scripture I heard in church.

But which deep am I meant to answer?

Within the cocoon of darkness, there was no pain, no despair. Just cold darkness. I feel if Dr. Reed was here right now, she would make some analogous statement between how the darkness being cold and shallow represents my heart and mind at this point. But who's got time for that right now?

Although I love the darkness, I often feel a duplicitous nature within myself. Being unseen has provided me an opportunity to observe the world and exist and be invisible all at the same time. This duplicitous nature has become me, and I have become it.

Overall, I'm a good person, if I do say so myself. But one could not help but note that someone such as myself, who has experienced so many horrors of life, who has both tasted and experienced trauma and blood, could possibly transform themselves into that particular person or thing. Could I one day become like Senior? Will I develop a lust for torture and torment? Will this darkness that shrouds me be a gateway to the world that I so desperately want to evade?

As I lay there, I begin to reminisce about church service. I could hear the boisterous voice of Evangelist Sterns, as she sang "Washed Under the Blood." One of the lyrics was: "Washed under the blood of the crucified Lamb, I am all that God said I am."

As those lyrics kept replaying in my mind, it was like a light pierced through the darkness. As I lay there on my back looking up at the ceiling, I felt a presence come over me. A weight lifted from my eyes. Tears began to flow, and I began singing the song: "I am all that God said I am."

I felt and saw a light shine over me. The darkness and its imaginations departed and disappeared; they couldn't comprehend the light. I lifted my arms to touch the light and said what was on my heart. It wasn't some elaborate sermon or speech or even any prophetic words. All I said was, "Yes, Lord." I fell asleep.

Over the next few weeks, I began to attend church more. I would go on Wednesday nights for Bible study. I even joined the choir, where I would stand right next to the phenomenal Evangelist Sterns. I continued going to Friday night services and even got FaLessia to come with me sometimes.

We would often have food for sale, and I would go into the kitchen and help cook. This was the beginning of my love of nachos. Many people came Friday night not for the music, but for the prophecy service and the nachos.

One Sunday, Pastor Pressley gave a rousing sermon and lit the church up. So many people caught the Holy Ghost. It was a great day at church. At the end of her sermon, she looked over at me and said, "Brother Mario, the Lord is showing me a woman, and she is draped in a white gown, and a light from Heaven is shining on you, and this robe came over you."

And it was like that night a couple weeks ago when I felt this light illuminating over me—a warmth and coolness at the same time. It was welcoming, almost reminiscent of when I stood up at church as a little kid to get baptized. Tears filled my eyes.

I felt so disarmed—all my walls and shielding were washing away as each tear streaked across my face. I arose and began to walk towards the front of the church. Each step is heavy, each step is determined, each step is difficult. I felt like a baby gazelle taking its first steps. I wanted to just lay at the altar—the ultimate act of surrender. I'd gone too long, fought too hard. My way was not getting it done. Maybe if I surrendered unto God, I would be better. I would be renewed. A new birth could happen within my life.

I stood there at the altar, my legs trembling like a newborn colt, peering into the eyes of the prophetess, the pastor. Her eyes weren't just looking at me—they were seeing *through* me, past the broken boy, past the trauma, past the shame, straight into the man God intended me to be. Those eyes blazed like twin flames, and I felt exposed, seen, and loved all at once.

Then, like a sacred dance choreographed by Heaven itself, a crowd of ministers began to encircle me. An elder to my left, his weathered hands already lifted in prayer. One of the church mothers to my right, tears streaming down her aged cheeks as she whispered, "Yes, Lord, yes, Lord." A minister behind me, his deep voice humming an old hymn that seemed to vibrate through my bones.

The church didn't just erupt—it exploded. What had been praise transformed into something otherworldly. Voices lifted like thunder rolling across celestial plains. Hands clapped in rhythm that seemed to match the very heartbeat of God. Feet stomped against worn wooden floors until the entire sanctuary trembled with the holy earthquake.

One of the church sisters was shouting now, her voice cutting through the cacophony like a sword of praise: "Somebody's getting delivered tonight! Somebody's chains are breaking!" The congregation responded in waves of "Yes! Hallelujah! Thank you, Jesus!"

The piano—oh, that piano—fingers flew across those keys like someone was typing a love letter directly to Heaven. The bass notes thundered through the floorboards, up through my feet, into my chest, until my very heartbeat synchronized with the rhythm of redemption. The higher notes soared above us all, carrying our praise straight to the Throne Room.

The organ joined in, its voice deep and ancient, filling every corner of the sanctuary with sound so rich you could taste it. The drums kicked in—boom, boom, BOOM—matching the pulse of every heart in that place, until we weren't just worshipping together, we were breathing together, existing together as one body crying out for the same salvation.

All around me, the congregation had become a symphony of surrender. Someone was speaking in tongues, their voice liquid and musical. A deacon was waving his handkerchief like a flag of victory. A young woman was dancing in the aisles, her feet barely touching the ground as she moved to music only she could hear.

And through it all, the prophetess's eyes never left mine, anchoring me in that moment, holding me steady as everything I'd ever known about myself began to crumble and rebuild simultaneously.

This is it. Here I stand, surrendering, yielding a pound of flesh for spirit, sacrifice for salvation, rage for redemption, past for praise, worry for worship, and ghosts for God.

I wondered what my cost for salvation would be, but then I remembered hearing a Word in church that said the sacrifices of God are a broken spirit, a broken and contrite heart. And that is what I offered that day—uninhibited, raw Mario.

I looked in the eyes of the prophetess pastor, looking beyond her to the cross on the wall, and in my spirit, I said, *"Here I am, Lord."*

Immediately, she placed her hand on my forehead. I could smell the olive oil on her hands, anointed oil that she used, and she began to pray. The deacons rushed to the altar as my knees began to give out. She prayed harder and harder as I slipped down, falling to the altar.

I lay there—a lamb for the slaughter, a lamb as a sacrifice unto God. But what I began to learn, or rather would learn later on, is that Jesus paid the cost. He was the perfect lamb. He stood in my place so I didn't have to die. My goal was to accept Him and rise from the torrents of life and become a new creature in Christ.

As she released her hand from my head, I sprung up, and for the first time, joy encompassed me. I began, like the old folks were saying, to shout and praise.

Now I am no small-frame guy—at about 6 feet, 350-plus pounds—so all the women ministers quickly got out of my way. Since this was an older church, all the deacons were well in their sixties, so it was rather difficult to contain me as I shouted all through the front of the church.

I never understood the saying, "joy unspeakable," but at that moment, I didn't have a care in the world. In that moment, a newness was coming about in me—one in which I could see the unknown future, one in which pain would be replaced with purpose, and purpose defined and sketched out in my heart. One in which I was both uncertain and glad about.

This type of duality, this type of duplicitousness, is what I needed in my life.

The pastor glided back to the pulpit with the grace of someone who had witnessed a miracle. She gripped the mahogany edges, her knuckles white with holy intensity, and her voice rang through the sanctuary like a bell announcing victory: "Church! Church! We have a new brother in Christ tonight! Brother Mario has accepted Jesus as his Lord and Savior!"

The congregation exploded again, but this time it was pure celebration. Handkerchiefs waved like flags of surrender. Hands clapped with thunderous approval. Voices shouted praise that seemed to shake the very foundations of the building.

"Now church," the pastor continued, her voice cutting through the jubilation, "y'all know what time it is! Let's welcome our brother home!"

She raised her arms, and like a conductor before a celestial orchestra, led the entire congregation in the traditional call and response: "Let the church say amen!"

"AMEN!" came the unified roar, a sound so powerful it seemed to push against the walls of the sanctuary.

"Let the church say amen!"

"AMEN!" Even louder this time, voices layering upon voices, creating harmonies that had never been rehearsed but felt ancient and eternal.

"Let the church say amen!"

"AMEN! AMEN! AMEN!"

The chant took on a life of its own, each "amen" building upon the last, creating a rhythm that pulsed through the floorboards and into our very souls. Some voices were high and sweet, others deep and resonant, but all united in this one word that meant "so be it" and, "yes, Lord" and, "we agree with Heaven."

Then, rising above the symphony of amens like a phoenix taking flight, came the voice that could silence storms and wake the dead. Evangelist Sterns stepped forward, and when she opened her mouth, the very air seemed to catch fire. Her voice wasn't only heard—it was felt, experienced, lived. It rolled through the sanctuary like thunder announcing the presence of the Almighty, yet it carried the tenderness of a mother's lullaby.

She began to sing, and I swear the angels themselves leaned down from Glory to listen. Her voice commanded not only attention, but reverence. Every demon within a hundred miles must have fled at the sound, because what emanated from her throat was pure Heaven distilled into melody. The words she sang wrapped around each person in that sanctuary like individual love letters from God Himself.

The congregation swayed as one body, caught up in the current of her praise. Some wept openly. Others raised their hands toward Heaven. A few stood in stunned silence, overwhelmed by the beauty of what they were witnessing.

And in that moment, as Evangelist Sterns's voice painted pictures of grace and redemption in the air around us, I understood what it meant to be welcomed home by the Family of God.

I took my seat, and like Jesus, I wept.

Chapter 11: FEAR = False Evidence Appearing Real

"You're making some real progress," Dr. Reed states. She peers over her glasses and jots down more notes. This is one of the few times that I look forward to meeting her.

Life has been on the upswing since rejoining church. I feel so purposeful, like my life has some meaning. *Have you ever just been alive and felt like you existed? Like life is happening all around you and you are nothing more than a mere spectator? Never involved, just watching?* I carried myself through life feeling that way—and I used that phrase correctly, "carried myself"—because all the time it was a struggle. I know now that it was God who carried me. But it still felt like a struggle.

Outside of church, I've been leaning on my new friend group. We even started a book club called Turning Pages, which was a play on most of our job titles as I was a page at the Flint Public Library.

I love books. I've always idolized going to the library. It's the physical manifestation or representation of knowledge, and I've always been someone striving for knowledge. To walk down the aisles of the library, the stacks of books represent majestic aisles in some royal priesthood.

"Now I know there's a lot of things going on in your life right now, but I don't want us to get too far off of our assignment here," Dr. Reed interjects. "Remember I said we must do the work." She sits back in her chair and locks eyes with me.

Yeah, so much for my trip down memory lane, I guess. "I don't know, Doctor. I feel like I'm healed." I clasp my hands together and give her a slight smile.

Her face remains unchanging, her demeanor straightforward. She sat in silence for a few seconds, which felt like hours.

"I don't want you to be so caught up in the good moments that you forget that life shifts up and down, back and forth, in and out. I need to make sure you are equipped to handle the ebb and flow of life."

Why does she have to ruin a good thing?

"I don't want to take away from your moment, and I know this is a good time for you. But we must continue to work. We must continue pulling all these layers so we can get to the root of the issues and find that bountiful purpose for life."

"Fine," I resigned, sitting back in the chair uncomfortably. I shoot her a stern, directed look.

Unwavering in her position, she locks eyes with me. "You rarely talk about your love life. Why is that?" Her tone and question throw me off. *Where are we going with this?* "You've been working on so many issues in this department. I want to make sure that you're open—you can't let your experiences and trauma affect you going forward."

She pauses, and instinctively I lean forward as if she's about to tell me some mysterious life secret, like the key to my future that will unlock it as well as lock my past lies just beyond her lips, carried out on the breath of her voice. I wait with bated breath.

"You seem so broken sometimes. Even during your good times, you always seem broken. However, I want you to know that one day somebody's going to hug you so tight that they're going to push all the broken pieces together for you. You mentioned going on this date to this Millionaire's Ball—sounds great. Tell me about it."

This was the first time I saw glee creep across the face of Dr. Reed, but I hate to burst her bubble.

"Ummm," I stagger over the words. "Me and FaLessia were *not* on a date."

A smirk etches across her face. "Oh really?" she says matter-of-factly. "Did you buy the tickets, rent a car, and ask her to go with you?"

I nodded, shuffling slightly uncomfortable in my seat. "She's a great friend of mine, and it was just two friends enjoying the evening."

She slightly rolls her eyes in a playful fashion. "If that's what you want to call it—they used to call this courting," she states as she repositions herself in her chair. "So, did you have fun on this date? I mean," she clears her throat, "this evening with a *friend*?"

Her mocking tone was not lost on me. This was yet another breach of decorum for the doc. *Touché*.

Memory: The Millionaire's Ball

The Millionaire's Ball was an event hosted by my church. We gathered dressed up in our finest clothes and had a grand time. The more affluent members of the church rented limos, but on my budget, I rented one of my dream cars, which was an early 2000 Grand Prix. I rented a dapper suit to fit the colors of the night, purple and gold.

I remember picking up FaLessia, and she was super excited to join us. She looked quite beautiful. The organizers had picked an excellent hall and here were so many people. The event, perfectly matching the theme, was decorated with vibrant shades of purple and gold.

Crystal chandeliers hung from the vaulted ceiling like frozen fireworks, casting prisms of light across the room that danced on every surface. Each round table was draped in rich purple linens with gold charger plates that caught the light and reflected it back like small suns. Towering centerpieces of purple orchids and white roses spilled from golden vases, their fragrance mixing with the subtle scent of expensive perfume and cologne that floated through the air.

Purple and gold fabric was draped elegantly from the ceiling, creating an almost tent-like canopy effect that made the entire space feel intimate despite its grandeur. Gold-rimmed glasses caught the light at each place setting, and the silverware gleamed like it had never been used.

Even the napkins were folded into perfect roses, each one tied with a golden ribbon.

The stage at the front was adorned with cascading purple curtains and gold trim, while uplighting bathed the walls in alternating hues of royal purple and warm gold. Balloon arrangements in matching colors created archways at the entrance, and the dance floor seemed to shimmer under the rotating disco ball that cast tiny stars across the room.

Everything sparkled, everything gleamed, everything whispered of elegance and wealth. It was the kind of place where fairytales happened, where Cinderella might have danced with her prince.

For a moment, I felt like I was in the wrong spot. No one such as myself, coming from where I've come from, would ever be at such an event unless to clean or cook for it. There was music, food, dancing, and raffles. It was pleasant.

I remember dropping her off. She looked quite nervous. But as we sat in her mother's driveway, as I was saying my goodbyes, I blurted out, "You know this wasn't a date, right?"

She looked shocked. "Of course."

Years later, I learned those words hurt her feelings. But I was naive and didn't know.

"Sounds like this was a really good evening, and you really enjoyed your date? I mean, *friend*," Dr. Reed stated. And yes, I caught all the shade.

"The thought of me getting involved in any type of romantic relationship at this point is far-reaching. I pretty much closed myself off to that idea. The overarching feeling and mantra, if you will, for my life centered around 'everybody leaves me'—a perpetuating fear that I always have."

"Mario, you can't be closed off with the fear that somebody's going to leave you. You must be open to the idea that God wants you to have love. He wants you to feel that love. Remember, the Bible says that God is love. I've always thought that experiencing love as a human is one of the closest points we can get to actually touching the Face of our Creator."

That thought resonated with me, albeit not enough for me to consider any type of romantic relationship. But a tiny part of me welcomed the thought.

"I think you have classic abandonment syndrome." I shift in my chair with a confused look on my face.

"People who go through trauma like you have typically throw up these walls and embrace a form of isolation. Now the question I have for you is: are you healing, or are you just isolating yourself from the trauma? There's a difference."

Could she be correct? Am I on this healing journey, but is it truly healing, or is it just isolation? Is it true that two warring countries are at peace because they don't speak? Or are they at peace because there is no interaction? What happens when we interact?

Fast Forward Ten Years

"Hey."

I stood in the doorway, half teary-eyed, half stunned. *Oh, how the mighty have fallen.* He was a relic, a giant, a Goliath whose David was time and food. I stood there witnessing Senior bedridden, forcing life into his body with labored breath. He is a mess of about 500 to 600 pounds.

Pity rose up in me as I stood there in the doorway, with Junior ushering me in, saying, "Come on, Mario. Go say hi to Dad."

I was comfortable with him being a relic, but the sound of Junior's voice awakened him, and I saw a shift in his eyes. Slight movements from his arms and legs let me know there was still life within his body. The room smelled of feces and urine, and the stench of evil. It was encamped, the prison that held him. The only light emanating from a crack within the curtains.

He looks over at me, and pity is immediately replaced with fear.

"Hey, boy," he says in a growl. His voice sent chills up my spine. I couldn't move.

"Hi," I weakly said.

"Well, don't just stand there. Come on in," he commands and instructs Junior to turn on the lights and the TV.

"Hey, Pop, I brought Mario and his kids so that you can see them since you never seen them," Junior states as he acquiesces to his commands and prepares the room.

Behind me were my two twin boys, Jace and Jaiden, peering around me, eager to see this "bad man" they'd heard their father mention. But what they saw was an elderly, obese man who seemed harmless to them.

"We brought you some food," I weakly state, stuttering with each word.

He instructs Junior to retrieve the food and put it up. His eyes center upon my two boys. For a moment, I saw joy creep across his face. *Could he be happy?*

"Look at you boys. Come on in here and give your granddad a hug."

The boys rush to hug him. In their minds, this is their grandfather, much like their maternal grandfather, Charles Howard, who was an utter saint in their eyes. Senior had to be the same. As anyone who has kids knows, sometimes your kids think you make a big deal out of nothing.

As for me, at that moment, I stood there witnessing. And as the Bible says, watch as well as pray.

Senior had always had a performative power. It was almost like a switch on the wall with him. He could turn on the charm and portray an image that would be so compelling that others wouldn't dare to even see the real him—the one that I grew up with, the monster.

He always had the ability to create a narrative that the issues between us were one-sided. It was always *me, my* exaggeration, *my* attitude that kept me away from him for many, many years. No matter the bruises, my recollection, my pleas, my word and my truth were never good enough for almost anyone in my life. My testimony was never sufficient. It always paled in comparison to his charm.

Even when we tried to reconnect years ago, he manipulated text messages. He would send me a text saying, "Hey son, I love you. How is your day going?" And I would respond, "Thanks for reaching out, my day is going well."

The next day, he'd respond, "Well, I guess you're still mad at me, but I'm gonna continue to reach out."

My response back to him: "I did respond. I told you I was doing well. What's going on?"

A couple days later: "I see that you're still not talking to me. But I love you, and whenever you're ready, text me back."

I would then respond, "Not sure what's going on. Maybe you're not getting my text messages. I even tried to call you and you didn't answer. I left you a couple of voicemail messages. I thought we were moving forward."

He never called me back or responded any further, so I let it die.

Two weeks later, me and Junior were out shopping. As I was going to my car, he brought it up.

"With you being in church, I would think you would be putting more of an effort to get back together with Dad."

I turned quickly and confronted him aggressively. Anyone who knows me at this point knows that bringing up this man to me is asking for an argument.

"What do you mean?" I demanded.

"Yeah, Dad showed me the text messages. He's reaching out to you and you're not even responding to him."

"What the—" I thought. "I respond to every one of his text messages and I call him. What are you talking about?"

He counters me. "I've seen the text messages. He has been reaching out to you and you don't respond. You need to stop being a hypocrite in the church. And if you're truly going to forgive him, you need to forgive him."

I guess the battle was set for the parking lot of Sam's Club. I dropped decorum and propriety.

"First, you are not, nor is your father, anyone that I will ever have to lie to. If I said it is so, **it is so.** I don't believe in casually lying because I have no fear and nothing to gain from it. I don't know where you get your information from, but it's clearly false. Don't come to me unless you have true facts. You've had all day to talk to me about something—don't wait and do it here. You think I won't act a fool in this parking lot, but you are mistaken."

I drop my groceries and approach him within inches of his face. *Let's do it.*

He takes a step back. "Mario, I've seen the text messages."

"Oh really? You have?" I whipped out my phone, quickly go through the text exchange and showed him.

For several moments he scanned through my phone. Satisfaction and enjoyment rose up in me as I watched him come to the realization of what I'd always told him. This was the one moment at which he could not deny my testimony or my truth. His father was a lying, deceitful manipulator.

His jaw dropped. "Wait a minute. You're responding. And he's responding back like you're not responding. I saw his phone—the only thing I saw was his messages to you. No responses."

I look at him and shake my head. "I told you this man is a liar. You know who he truly is, but you deny the truth. What you gonna do with the facts here right in front of you? He clearly has been deleting my responses so that he can show you and get a pity party from you and carry on the narrative that Mario is the problem. And you, like everybody else in the family, treat me and act like I am. But you have your proof. You see it? I doubt you're gonna do anything with it. I'm gonna pack up and go. I'll talk to you whenever."

He tries to stop me, but to no avail. I pack up my groceries, get in my car, and drive home.

The Devastating Realization

And what I'm witnessing here with my own kids is the exact thing that he's capable of doing and does. He is skillful in his craft, direct in his demeanor, and resolute in his deceit. Well played, Sir.

The children are thoroughly enjoying spending time with their new grandfather. And as usual, I relegate myself to the background. But an unfamiliar feeling rises in me, and I'm confounded by it.

Jealousy.

I'm not jealous of anyone, but for a moment there, seeing him interact with my children, I became jealous. Now I have long since learned to exist without his love and acceptance. I survived off tears and pittance. But I've always viewed him as someone who was incapable of love and affection. *He only had enough to give to Junior, right? He couldn't love another child.* He couldn't be affectionate with anyone else. He couldn't be a father to me and to Junior.

But to see how soft he was with my children, how loving and kind—I wish I had that experience.

And the realization I had in that moment broke me at the foundation.

It wasn't that he wasn't capable. **He made a decision.** He decided I wasn't worthy of those feelings, that acceptance and that love. Here on display, he shows he has it and can give it. And in my mind, I reason that there was something unlovable about me, which caused him to not want or deem me not worthy of receiving from him.

The pain I felt in realizing his actions were intentional hurt more than any physical confinement ever could.

I left the room to go to the kitchen because I was feeling overwhelmed. Within a few minutes, the boys came out to hug me. They knew their dad was having a difficult time. Funny that two six-year-olds can pick up something that the adults couldn't.

While the kids played, nostalgia washed over me as I revisited the house where I was born. It seemed smaller than I remembered, but familiar features like the living room and dining table were unchanged despite all that hadshifted.

I was enjoying this trip down memory lane until I looked at a wall and noticed the shoddy patchwork that was done. I remembered that this was probably one of the holes in the wall that he put there with either a fist or my mother's head.

Let me take a detour from this trip down memory lane...

And as I exited this memory, I heard raised voices coming from the bedroom. Senior and Junior were at it again. They transitioned beyond father and son to friends after the divorce from my mother, so it was very common for them to get into arguments. But this time was different to me.

I heard threats being issued, cussing. One of the things that I heard stopped me in my tracks. Senior yelled, "Say one more thing and I'm going to fuck you up!"

My heart leapt into my chest. I stood there, stolid and frozen within my steps. My breathing matched the pace of my heart.

Now, I know some people will think this is crazy. *Like, he's in a bed. He's bedridden, Mario. There's nothing he can do.* But the sheer fear alone of hearing my abuser's voice in the threatening tone that I've become all too familiar with froze me.

I remember an almost petrifying fear where I almost urinated on myself. I couldn't move. In this moment, I felt I failed as a father. I was so afraid and frozen that I couldn't even go and check and make sure my children were okay. My job was to make sure they were okay. And at that moment, all I could think about was how afraid I was and how I would not go into that room.

I wanted to. In my mind, my feet were moving, but they were frozen.

Tears started running down my face, and I looked around the kitchen and saw a knife on the counter. I grabbed it and forced my legs to move. I heard him yelling again, and I shook my head and dropped the knife.

I wasn't David at that moment. I couldn't slay Goliath.

It is hard for many people to understand that, but I have been trained, programmed if you will, to I could never lay a hand on him. The thought was so foreign to me. *This is one thing you don't do: you don't hit Senior. You don't take action against him.*

Sadly, even as a man in his thirties, if he had told me to come in and lay across the bed and take a beating, I would have. I didn't have a choice.

The boys ran into the kitchen laughing and playing. *They're safe.* I breathe out. They come and give me a hug, and they look back at the door.

"Hey, Dad, Uncle and Granddad are fighting."

I nod my head, wipe away my tears, and sniffle. "I know, son, I know."

I ushered them to the door. Like Tina running from Ike, we rushed to our car, and I attempted to flee.

Junior met me at the car. "Hey, wait, where are you going?"

"I gotta get the hell outta here. Bye." And I peel off.

Back to Reality

"Mario," Dr. Reed says, "when I say isolation in relation to healing, it's all a part of something called Stockholm Syndrome. You might have experienced this many times in your life and not even be aware of it. What you experienced in your life was psychological manipulation accompanied by prolonged captivity. Some of the survival instincts that the brain may adapt are ways in which you can reduce perceived threats and increase your chances of survival—and isolation is one of them. You avoid these situations so that you are not in danger, so that your survival is perceived as guaranteed. You're not per se healed but rather protected by your own isolation."

She leans forward. "And I'm not saying this is bad either. You must make the best decision about what's best for your life. If avoidance and isolation is best for you, then do that. All my fancy degrees"—she waved her hand towards the wall where of all her degrees were prominently displayed—"can't advise you that you are supposed to encounter danger and deal with it at that moment. You must develop a plan that is best for you. I would do you a disservice to tell you otherwise."

"The Scripture tells us that God has not given us the spirit of fear, but of power, love, and sound mind. And I heard before that fear is **false** **e**vidence **a**ppearing **r**eal. You have power. You have love. And you have a sound mind. Although your mind is hurt right now, you are coping the best that you can. What I don't want you to do is continue to allow fear to grip and hold you."

"I want to say that Senior leaving created this abandonment issue that you have, which in turn created this attachment issue that you have. Let's talk about when he left. What did that do for you?"

And this was the first time I realized that Dr. Reed had it wrong. Him leaving was not a sad day for me at all, but it was a day of freedom for me. Maybe I did develop some attachment issues, but abandonment issues? I think she has it wrong.

The timer rings, signaling the end of our session.

"Well, typically that means that we're done for the day, but I don't have another appointment and we can definitely go ahead and talk about these abandonment issues."

I look at Dr. Reed and say, "That's all the time we have today, Dr. Reed. Let's pick this up next session." I stand.

She looks perplexed and amused at the same time. "Yes, Mario, we will indeed pick this up."

I exit through the door and look back at the nameplate on the door: Dr. S. Reed. I take a deep breath, and dread builds up knowing that our next session is going to talk about when the Goliath was not slain, but fled.

Chapter 12: When Goliath Fled

In the Bible, the young shepherd David faced Goliath, a nine-foot Philistine giant terrorizing Israel's army. While seasoned warriors cowered, David stepped forward with only a sling and five smooth stones. "You come with sword and spear, but I come in the Name of the Lord," he declared. With perfect aim, David's stone struck Goliath's forehead, felling the giant instantly. David then used Goliath's own sword to finish him, proving that faith conquers fear.

But what happens if David didn't slay Goliath, but instead Goliath flees?

Memory: Mama's Missing

It was a normal day in the Booker household—well, *our* normal. Mama had to get to work, leaving me and Junior there with Senior. Although normal, there was a tinge of apprehension and something else I couldn't quite explain that lingered in the air. Nevertheless, no arguments, no fighting—I'll take it.

Me and Junior played in the backyard. It was a mid-spring afternoon. We chased each other around the backyard and played with the forts we made with milk crates, and our GI Joes. And then, abruptly, charging through the backyard with grave authority reserved for someone embodying the attitude and attributes of a slaveholder, Senior stormed toward us.

"Y'all stop. You're going over to your auntie's house," he commanded and returned to the house.

I know that when Mama isn't around, he's typically itchy for some reason to get upset and cause some turmoil in the house. Although the idea of being around this particular aunt didn't sit too well with me, at least I'd get to see my cousins. It wasn't that I didn't love her. I did. It was the inconsistent mood shifts and attitudes that made me feel unwelcome. But my mother loved her younger sister.

Before leaving, my grandfather showed up. He was a stern but beloved figure, and I loved seeing him. He was a tall, caramel-complexioned, gray-haired gentleman. Although I heard stories about his rougher days, he was nothing but kind to me, and with my experiences, I appreciated anyone who showed me kindness.

The drive to her house was uneventful, very normal. We traveled down Clio Road, passing the familiar landmarks of inner-city Flint—Mike's Coney Island with its hand-painted sign barely hanging on, Shirley's Hair Palace with women sitting under dryers visible through the large windows, the corner liquor store with bars on the windows and men clustered outside, and the Church's Chicken that always had a line of cars wrapped around the building. The neighborhoods got progressively rougher as we headed north, houses with boarded-up windows mixed in with ones where families sat on porches trying to catch any breeze they could find.

Arriving on Hobson Avenue, the street pulsed with life—a symphony of urban summer activity that felt worlds away from the tension at home. Kids darted between parked cars like schools of fish, their voices creating a constant backdrop of laughter and playful arguments. A group of girls jumped Double Dutch on the sidewalk, their coordinated feet creating rhythmic percussion against the concrete while they chanted songs that echoed off the narrow houses. Boys rode bikes in wide circles, popping wheelies and showing off for anyone who'd watch, their bike chains clicking and wheels spinning against the asphalt.

The porches served as outdoor living rooms where grandmothers sat in lawn chairs, fanning themselves with church fans while keeping watchful eyes on the children. Their conversations floated through the air—discussions about church services, neighborhood gossip, and who was cooking what for Sunday dinner. The smell of barbecue drifted from someone's backyard, mixing with the scent of honeysuckle climbing up the chain-link fences that divided the small yards.

An ice cream truck meandered down the street, its distorted melody drawing children from every direction like a Pied Piper. The driver, a patient man who knew every kid's name and their usual order, handed out rocket pops and ice cream sandwiches with the practiced ease of someone who'd been working in this neighborhood for years. The truck's presence transformed the street into a temporary festival, with kids negotiating with parents for money and debating the merits of different frozen treats.

We pulled into the driveway, and my cousins circled the car like a swarm of bees, their faces lighting up with genuine excitement. They peppered us with questions before we could even get out—

"Y'all staying for dinner?"

"Did you bring any games?"

"Can we go to the store later?"

My aunt appeared in the doorway, wiping her hands on a dish towel, her expression warm but slightly puzzled by our unexpected arrival.

Senior looked back and says, "Alright, see you later," not acknowledging my aunt or cousins. He left. I thought it was rude, but par for the course with him.

Through the course of the afternoon, we immersed ourselves in the vibrant chaos of extended family life. The house buzzed with activity—cousins ranging from toddlers to teenagers, each with their own personality and energy. We played video games on an old Nintendo system; the controllers passed around in careful rotation to avoid arguments. The older cousins taught us card games on the front porch, while the younger ones demanded attention with constant streams of knock-knock jokes and made-up stories.

The afternoon light filtered through sheer curtains, casting patterns across the well-worn furniture that told stories of family gatherings, holiday celebrations, and countless ordinary moments. Photo albums lay scattered on the coffee table, filled with pictures of family reunions, school graduations, and church events—visual proof of connections and continuity that felt both comforting and foreign to my experience at home.

It was a nice reprieve, but I couldn't shake that feeling in the atmosphere, something unspoken hovered just beyond the laughter and normal family rhythms.

It started getting late, and I knew Mama was off work and it was dinnertime, so I knew she was cooking as she always did. But typically, we would be home getting things around the house together before we sat down and ate. She never would get off work and not see us.

One aunt asked, "Has anyone heard from Jean?" She gave her sister a meaningful look, hinting at a private conversation. When they went inside, I tried to listen in from the stairs but couldn't catch what they were saying. After some phone calls and whispers, I pretended to use the restroom to get closer, but when I entered, everyone went silent.

"Mario, what do you need?"

"I gotta use the bathroom," I stated.

"Well, hurry up and head back outside. Your mom's on her way to pick you up."

False alarm, I thought. *Mom's okay.*

The Arrival

Now Miss Emma Jean has always had a way about herself. She was known as "Sweet Jean." We all knew when my mother hit the block—she had a fiery red Camaro, and she was not afraid of hitting the gas pedal. She would burn rubber down the street, blasting blues music for no particular reason, and today was no exception. She peeled in front of the house, waved at her sister in acknowledgment, and commanded us to get into the car.

It was a strange car ride because Mother was never one to be quiet, and whenever we tried small talk, she either ignored us or barely responded. She gripped the steering wheel with such determination I was for a moment concerned that we were gonna get into an accident.

We peeled into the house on Keller Street, and I noticed that Senior was not home. *Good. We could eat dinner, watch TV, and chill out with no issues.*

When we entered the home, I was in total shock.

We were not rich by any means, but our house was furnished with antiques and regal furniture from my maternal great-grandfather and his wife, who worked in steel factories and moved from Louisiana to Michigan. He bought up properties for him and his wife and their daughter, my grandmother, Dorine Hawthorne Booker.

We had big, fancy China cabinets that held antique cutlery, and gold-rimmed plates. We even had fancy little knickknacks scattered throughout the house and luxury couches. But when we walked in, everything was gone. The only things left were a chair and the dining room table.

We looked through the house—all our belongings remained, but the only things that were missing were the items from the house and Senior 's belongings. He took dishes, glasses, furniture, food from the pantries, and expensive items from the garage. He even cleaned out the safe that he and my mother had, including my grandfather's precious antique coin collection—Mercury dimes, Indian head pennies, and silver dollars that had been passed down through generations, each coin representing decades of family history and financial security that my grandfather had carefully preserved.

I tried to go to the basement to see what was left, and the lights didn't work. I raced to the room to talk to Mother, and she sat on the bed with her hands covering her face, crying, and Junior sat next to her crying also.

"Mama, the lights don't work."

"Your father turned the power off also. He took everything. *Everything.*"

We began canvassing the house, taking an inventory of what we had left: big screen TV gone, microwave gone, VCR gone, power turned off, money from safe gone, grandfather's coin collection gone, and most importantly, Senior gone.

Mama's Meltdown

What happened next was something I'd never seen before and never wanted to see again.

Mama collapsed onto the bare wooden floor of what used to be our living room, her knees hitting hard against the oak boards. The sound echoed through the empty space like a gunshot. She began to wail—not cry, not sob, but wail like something deep inside her soul had been ripped apart with jagged edges.

Her hands clawed at the floor as if she was trying to dig her way out of this nightmare. Tears streamed down her face in rivers, and her whole body convulsed with each breath she tried to take. She rocked back and forth; her arms wrapped around herself like she was trying to hold the pieces together.

"How could he do this? How could he do this to us?" she kept repeating, her voice getting higher and more hysterical with each repetition. "Twelve years! Twelve years of my life! Twelve years!"

She tried to stand but stumbled, catching herself against the wall where the China cabinet used to be. The empty space seemed to mock her, and she slammed her fist against the wall over and over until her knuckles started bleeding.

"He took my grandfather's coins! *My* grandfather's coins!" she screamed, sliding down the wall until she was crumpled on the floor again. "Those were all I had left of him. All I had left!"

Junior tried to comfort her, but she was inconsolable. She kept looking around the empty room like she couldn't believe what she was seeing, like maybe if she looked hard enough, everything would reappear.

The worst part was when she got quiet. After all the screaming and crying, she sat there in silence, staring at nothing, her face blank except for the tears that kept falling. It was like watching someone die while they were still breathing.

My Response

I didn't quite understand why Mama was so upset. The source of so much pain and confusion in our lives—his exodus was almost like a prayer being answered. At that moment, I didn't grieve his loss. I didn't feel a loss.

Am I to grieve pain? Am I to grieve torment? These were things that I had that were gone when he left.

Although maybe not the best thought to have at that moment, I remember thinking that even though we didn't have any power and we'd have to try and figure out something to eat tonight, this may be the first night that I will get some peaceful sleep.

Before it started getting too dark, I found a couple of items that he left around the house, and I started collecting them and putting them into a box. Junior gave me an angry look and said, "So you're just gonna pack my dad's stuff up?"

I looked at him and said, "Sure is," and continued to pack up stuff.

My mom, still upset and enraged, got on the phone with her mother, telling her that I didn't even care and I'm packing up the rest of his belongings. My grandmother on the phone yelled at my mother to tell me she's gonna beat my ass and to stop packing up his stuff.

I ignored the threat and continued.

The monster, the tormentor, my Goliath was not slain, but he fled.

My mother grieved that night—the dissolution of her marriage, the loss that she experienced of material things, and the oncoming lack of substance this house would endure in the absence of Senior. At my age, my needs were immediate. I lacked the foresight she saw coming and how her life would ultimately change. She mourned the present and the future, but I rejoiced in the present as someone who I viewed as a tormentor had dramatically exited out of my life. Temporary or permanent, I was comfortable with it.

The Aftermath

We later found out that Senior moved in with his brother, and his father, brother, and friends helped him move all the belongings out of the house. I never understood why men got together to disenfranchise a family for the sake of friendship and manliness.

He kept his distance over several months. It got scary for a little bit of time because he refused to give the keys over, and we would come home sometimes and find evidence that somebody was in the house. He even threatened that one day he might come in and kill us all in our sleep.

One day he actually came to the house while we were away—not sure how he knew we were gone unless he was stalking the house—and we returned home to find the phone lines inside the house were ripped out and the food that my mother cooked in the refrigerator was eaten.

There was no use in calling the police because his brother was a lieutenant in the police office, and he had many friends. Each time my mother would call, they would ignore her requests for assistance. She eventually got the locks changed.

Dr. Reed's Analysis

Dr. Reed took no notes but looked at me intently. I met her gaze, not knowing what she was going to say.

"I can tell from your story that you felt bad for how you were feeling at that moment. What you went through over ten-plus years was bad—very bad. People grieve and handle situations differently, and in that moment, you saw a light at the end of the tunnel, and it gave you hope. Your mother and brother—the future she envisioned and the life that she built shattered before her eyes, and nothing she could do could change that. After everything that she suffered and went through, having dependency on him shattered her world. Your brother, having his idol leave, interrupted his version and image of life."

She leaned forward, her voice taking on a more clinical tone.

"What you experienced is called displacement—you displaced your need for safety and peace onto his absence. That's a healthy coping mechanism for a child in your situation. Your mother, however, was experiencing what we call trauma bonding and codependency syndrome. But Mario, there's something deeper we need to understand about your mother's response."

Dr. Reed paused, choosing her words with the precision of someone who had seen this pattern countless times.

"Your mother's devastation wasn't about losing a husband or even the material possessions. After twelve years of abuse, she had developed what we call 'survivor psychology.' She had unconsciously organized her entire sense of self around surviving his moods, his violence, his unpredictability. Every day, she woke up and her brain calculated: *How do I keep him calm? How do I protect my children? How do I manage his anger? How do I prevent the explosion?*"

She sat back, her expression growing more serious.

"This constant state of hypervigilance, this daily chess game of survival, had become her identity. She was extraordinarily skilled at reading his emotional temperature, at knowing when to speak and when to stay silent, at deflecting his rage away from you and your brother. These weren't weaknesses, Mario—they were survival skills that kept your family alive."

Dr. Reed's voice grew stronger.

"When he left, she didn't just lose her tormentor—she lost her purpose. Her entire nervous system had been calibrated to his presence, to managing the threat he represented. Without him there, she experienced what we call 'survivor's vertigo.' She no longer knew who she was or how to function when she wasn't in survival mode."

She leaned forward again, her eyes intense.

"Think about it—for twelve years, your mother's primary job was to be a human shield between his dysfunction and you children. She absorbed his anger, redirected his violence, negotiated for your safety every single day. She became a master strategist in the war zone of your home. When he left, she suddenly had no war to fight, no daily crisis to manage, no immediate threat to navigate around."

Dr. Reed opened her hands, as if releasing something.

"The coins, the furniture, the material losses—those were symbols of the security she thought she had earned through all those years of endurance. But more than that, they represented proof that her survival strategy had worked, that she had successfully maintained some stability despite the chaos. When he took those things, he was essentially telling her that all her years of careful management, all her sacrifice, all her strategic thinking had meant nothing."

She paused, letting that sink in.

"Your mother's breakdown wasn't just grief, Mario. It was the collapse of an entire identity that had been forged in trauma. She was experiencing what happens when someone who has been running on adrenaline and survival instincts for over a decade suddenly must figure out how to live in peace. Her nervous system didn't know how to process safety—it only knew how to process threats."

Dr. Reed sat back and opened her Bible.

"The Scripture tells us in Isaiah 43:19, 'Behold, I will do a new thing; now it shall spring forth; shall ye not know it? I will even make a way in the wilderness, and rivers in the desert.' Sometimes God must remove people from our lives—even people we think we need—to make room for the new thing He wants to do."

She looked directly at me.

"Your Goliath fled because God knew you needed freedom more than you needed the familiar dysfunction. Your mother's Goliath fled, and she experienced it as the death of everything she had learned to be. But God was making a way in the wilderness for both of you—you only saw it first because children often have clearer spiritual vision than adults who have been trapped in survival mode."

"The guilt you carry about feeling relieved needs to be released, Mario. You were not celebrating evil—you were celebrating freedom. There's nothing wrong with being grateful when oppression ends, even if it comes in a way that devastates people you love. Your mother's pain was real and valid—she was mourning the death of the woman she had to become to survive him. But your relief was equally real and valid—you were celebrating the birth of the boy you could become without him."

She closed the Bible and smiled gently.

"The question now is: how do you honor both your relief and your mother's complex grief? How do you move forward knowing that the same event that freed you also stripped away her entire sense of identity? The answer is grace—grace for yourself for feeling relief, grace for her for experiencing the terrifying freedom of no longer having to be a professional survivor, and grace for the fact that healing happens on different timelines for different people."

I sat there, feeling something shift inside me. For the first time, I didn't feel guilty about being glad he was gone. For the first time, I understood that my mother's devastation and my relief could coexist without one invalidating the other.

"Dr. Reed," I said slowly, "I never thought about it that way. I never understood that she had become someone completely different to protect us."

"Mario, your mother was a warrior who had been fighting a war for twelve years. When the war ended, she had to learn who she was in peacetime. That's one of the hardest transitions any human being can make. Your relief was a gift from God—a sign that your spirit recognized freedom when it came, even when it came wrapped in chaos."

She leaned forward once more.

"When Goliath fled, David still had to become king. Your freedom was only the beginning of your story, not the end of it. And your mother's collapse was just the beginning of her learning to be Emma Jean instead of Michael's target. The question is: what kind of man will you become with the life that his departure gave back to you? And how will you honor the woman who spent twelve years taking the hits meant for you?"

Chapter 13: Season of Growth

Two Years Later

The alarm at 6:30 AM doesn't feel like intrusion anymore—it feels like possibility. I roll out of bed in my one-bedroom apartment on the south side of Flint, the same complex where I lived during some of my darkest moments, but everything is different now. The shadows that once seemed to follow me everywhere have been replaced by something I never thought I'd experience: genuine optimism about the future.

I shower, dress in business casual attire—a far cry from the Kmart polo shirts that once defined my professional existence—and head to Sonitrol Security Systems, where I work as a Data Coordinator. The difference between analyzing security data and folding clothes or stocking shelves isn't just professional; it's psychological. Every day, I'm using my mind to solve problems, to create systems, to build something meaningful.

The drive to work takes me past ITT Technical Institute, where I completed my Associate of Applied Science degree in Network Administration. What should have been a celebration became a crisis when ITT suddenly closed when I was a few semesters away from completing my bachelor's degree. But God had other plans. He opened doors for me to continue my education at American Business and Technology University, pursuing a Bachelor's in Information Systems Engineering and Cybersecurity. Some nights after my online classes, I marvel at how God made a way when it seemed like all paths were blocked.

"Morning, Mario," calls Janet from the front desk as I walk into Sonitrol. She's become something of a work mother to me, always checking to make sure I'm eating lunch and asking about my classes.

"Morning, Janet. How was your weekend?"

"Can't complain. How are those classes going?"

"Network security exam on Thursday, but I think I'm ready for it."

"I know you are, honey. You're one of the smartest people in this building."

Two years ago, I wouldn't have believed her. Today, I smile and mean it when I say thank you.

My cubicle overlooks the parking lot, and as I boot up my computer to review overnight security alerts, I think about how Dr. Reed's words have proven prophetic. During our last session—we meet quarterly now instead of weekly, a testament to my progress—she told me something that has stuck with me:

"Mario, you're in your season of growth and development. The seed has been sown through all the work we've done together, through your commitment to healing, through your faith journey. Now it's time to reap."

She was right about the changing season. Work challenges that would have overwhelmed me two years ago now energize me. I find myself volunteering for additional projects, staying late not because I have to, but because I want to master every aspect of security systems and data analysis.

But the most significant growth isn't happening in the office or classroom—it's happening in my relationship with FaLessia.

The Evolution of Love

What started as a comfortable friendship has slowly, carefully, evolved into something I never thought I'd be capable of: a healthy romantic relationship. FaLessia and I have been officially dating for six months now, though the transition was so gradual that it's hard to pin-point exactly when "friends" became "more than friends."

The shift happened naturally, the way seasons change—impercepti-bly at first, then suddenly everything is different. It started with longer conversations after church, then coffee dates that weren't called dates, then her hand finding mine during prayer service. Unlike the dramatic, tumultuous relationship with the Unrequited Lover, this feels steady, safe, real.

FaLessia has this way of loving me that doesn't require me to per-form or prove my worth. She loves me in the light, proudly, openly. When we're together at church functions or family gatherings, she doesn't hide our relationship or act like she's embarrassed to be seen with me. It's the kind of love Dr. Reed always said I deserved but that I never believed was possible.

"You know what I love about you?" she told me just last week as we sat in her mother's living room after Sunday dinner.

"What's that?"

"You're not trying to be anyone else. You're just Mario. And Mario is enough."

The simplicity of that statement undid me. *Mario is enough.* Not Mario plus achievements, not Mario minus his past, not Mario perform-ing or pretending. Just Mario.

The Ring on the Dresser

Three weeks ago, after a particularly wonderful evening—dinner at Luigi's downtown, followed by a long drive through the countryside talking about everything and nothing—I made a decision that felt as natural as breathing.

I'd been carrying the ring in my pocket for two weeks, waiting for the "perfect moment" that never seemed to come. But as we pulled into her driveway and she headed inside to use the bathroom before I drove home, something clicked. *There didn't need to be orchestras or elabo-*

rate proposals. This relationship had been built on genuine moments, not grand gestures.

While she was in the bathroom, I took the ring box out of my pocket, opened it, and placed it on her bedroom dresser. Not dramatically, not with fanfare—just set it there like I might place down my keys.

When she came out and saw it, she screamed.

"MARIO DESEAN BOOKER, GET IN HERE RIGHT NOW!"

"Will you marry me?"

She looked at the ring, then at me, then back at the ring. Then she started laughing.

"Did you just put a ring on my dresser?"

"I...yes?"

She was full-on giggling now. "Baby, most people get down on one knee or take their girl somewhere romantic. You literally just set it on the dresser like it's the mail."

I felt my face burning with embarrassment. "I can do it differently—"

"Mario." She picked up the ring and looked at it, then at me. "This is perfect. This is so *you*. Yes, I'll marry you. But I'm telling this story for the rest of our lives!"

And she has been. Every time someone asks about our engagement, she grins and says, "He put the ring on the dresser. Just set it right there next to the meds and bills."

But what she always adds is this: "And that's how I knew it was real. He wasn't performing or putting on a show. He was just asking me to be his wife in the most honest way he knew how."

Building My Empire

"Empire" might seem like a strong word for a Data Coordinator position with an associate's degree in progress, but Dr. Reed taught me to think differently about success. My empire isn't measured in dollars or titles—it's measured in the distance I've traveled from where I started.

Two years ago, I was sleeping on a mattress in an empty house, unemployed, heartbroken, and convinced that everyone would eventually leave me. Today, I have a career with growth potential, I'm three semesters away from a degree, I'm engaged to a woman who loves me unconditionally, and I have a relationship with God that brings me peace instead of fear.

My empire is built on foundations that can't be shaken: self-worth that comes from God rather than from other people's approval, love that exists in the light instead of hiding in shadows, and a future that I'm actively creating instead of just surviving.

My supervisor, Mike Rodriguez, had been dangling a promotion in front of me for months. "Mario, you've got a mind for systems thinking," he told me repeatedly. "I'm going to promote you to Data Manager once we get through this merger."

I believed him. I worked overtime redesigning our entire Central Station following the company merger, streamlining operations and improving efficiency. I put my heart into that project, staying late, solving complex problems, creating something I was genuinely proud of. Mike praised my work publicly, telling upper management how valuable my contributions were.

The day after implementation was complete and the new system was running smoothly, Mike called me into his office.

"Mario, I'm sorry, but we have to let you go. Budget cuts from the merger."

I sat there stunned. "But you said you were *promoting* me. We just finished the project."

"I know, but things have changed. Corporate decision."

The betrayal cut deep. He had never intended to promote me. He had used the promise to keep me motivated through the redesign, then discarded me once he had what he needed. I had been played, manipulated, used—and it triggered every abandonment wound I thought I'd healed.

But God's timing is always perfect. Within two weeks, I landed a position as Account Manager for a global third-party logistics company. The role offered better pay, more growth potential, and the chance to work with international clients. What seemed like a devastating setback became a divine setup.

That night, I called FaLessia immediately, my voice heavy with disappointment and uncertainty.

"Baby, something happened at work today."

"What's wrong? I can hear it in your voice."

When I told her about the firing, she was quiet for a moment. Then she said something I'll never forget: "Mario, this isn't the end of your story. This is God closing a door so He can open a better one. We're going to get through this together."

Her unwavering support during those two weeks of job searching—when I could have easily spiraled back into old patterns of feeling worthless—showed me what real love looks like. She never once made me feel like less of a man for losing my job. Instead, she reminded me daily of my worth and capabilities.

When I got the call about the Account Manager position, she cried tears of joy. "I knew God would provide," she said, hugging me tightly. "He always does."

Dr. Reed's Wisdom

"You're reaping now, Mario," Dr. Reed said during our last session. "Everything we worked through—the trauma, the abandonment issues, the patterns of accepting less than you deserve—all of that work is bearing fruit."

She was right. The man who sits in her office today is fundamentally different from the broken boy who first walked through her doors. I can feel the difference in my bones.

"What's interesting," she continued, "is how all three areas of your life are growing simultaneously. Your career advancement, your healthy relationship with FaLessia, your continued spiritual growth—they're all feeding into each other."

"How so?"

"Your professional confidence is making you a better partner to FaLessia. Your secure relationship with her gives you the emotional stability to take risks in your career. Your spiritual foundation is providing the strength for both. It's a beautiful thing to witness."

She paused, looking at her notes from our early sessions.

"Do you remember when you first told me that everyone leaves you?"

"Of course."

"What do you believe now?"

I thought about FaLessia's unwavering support, about Mike's mentorship at work, about the church family that has embraced me, about Toni who still calls me her little brother even though we don't work together anymore.

"I believe that some people leave, but the right people stay. And I believe I'm worthy of people who stay."

Dr. Reed smiled. "That's not just healing, Mario. That's transformation."

The Foundation of Everything

Sunday mornings at In the Name of Jesus Full Gospel Church have become the anchor of my week. Pastor Pressley's sermons speak directly to my journey of restoration, and singing in the choir next to Evangelist Sterns still fills me with the same awe I felt that first night I gave my life to Christ.

But what's different now is that I'm not just attending church—I'm participating in the life of the church. I help with the Friday night nachos that everyone loves. I volunteer to drive elderly members to service when they need transportation. I've even been asked to share my testimony during a special service next month.

FaLessia has become as much a part of the church family as I am. She helps with the children's ministry and has developed a close relationship with Pastor Pressley. Watching her find her own spiritual path while supporting mine has been one of the most beautiful aspects of our relationship.

"Y'all are going to have a powerful ministry together," Pastor Pressley told us after service last Sunday. "God is preparing you for something special."

I don't know what that "something special" is yet, but I'm no longer afraid of God's plans for my life. The God I know now isn't the God of rubber hoses and Scripture beatings—He's the God who prepares tables in the presence of enemies, who makes beauty from ashes, who turns mourning into dancing.

Looking Forward

As I sit in my apartment tonight, working on an assignment for my network security class while FaLessia plans our wedding from her house across town, I'm struck by how ordinary and extraordinary my life has become.

Ordinary because I'm doing what millions of people do every day—working, going to school, planning a wedding, building a future.

Extraordinary because I'm doing it all despite odds that should have crushed me, despite a past that tried to convince me I was worthless, despite years of believing that I was unlovable and destined to be abandoned.

The little boy who was chained in basements and beaten with rubber hoses is still part of me, but he's no longer in the driver's seat. He's been healed, integrated, and transformed into strength. His pain has become my purpose; his trauma has become my testimony.

I'm 24 years old, engaged to my best friend, building a career that fulfills me, earning a degree, and walking in faith instead of fear.

Dr. Reed was right—this is my season of reaping.

And I have a feeling the harvest is just beginning.

Chapter 14: Stepping Stones

The sound of water cascading over rock has always brought me peace. Today, standing at Stepping Stone Falls in Flint, watching the Flint River flow over ancient stones worn smooth by time and persistence, I find myself drifting through memories like leaves on the current.

Seagulls cry overhead, their voices echoing off the water. The late afternoon sun catches the spray, creating tiny rainbows that appear and disappear with each shift of light. I've come here to think, to remember, to process the journey that brought me from broken boy to the man I am today.

My shadow stretches long across the path beside me, and I'm struck by the thought: I'm not alone anymore. God walks with me. Even my shadow is proof that light has found me.

A Winter Wedding

The memory crashes over me like the waterfall itself: my wedding day, nearly a decade ago. February 11th—a crisp winter morning that transformed into the brightest day of my life.

Victorian lilac and ivory was everywhere. The church sanctuary looked like something out of a fairytale, every pew adorned with silk ribbons and winter roses. Ice-blue uplighting cast ethereal shadows on the walls. Crystal snowflakes hung from invisible wire, catching the light and scattering it like promises across the ceiling.

But before any of that magic could happen, chaos struck at the worst possible moment.

The processional music had already started. The groomsmen were in position. I stood at the altar, heart pounding, waiting for my bride to appear. The musician played "Canon in D," and the guests turned expectantly toward the doors. Doors that remained firmly closed.

Inside the bride's room, panic reigned. FaLessia was ready—dressed, made up, bouquet in hand—but the door to enter the sanctuary was locked from the outside. Someone had accidentally engaged the lock when they left, and now my bride was trapped.

I could see Pastor Pressley whispering urgently to an usher, who rushed to find the janitor. The music played on. And on. The musician cycled through "Canon in D" twice, then improvised variations, then started looking at each other with increasingly worried glances.

From my position at the altar, I had no idea what was happening. I only knew my bride wasn't coming through those doors, and with each passing second, my mind conjured worse scenarios. *Did she change her mind? Did she run? Did something happen?*

Junior leaned over and whispered, "Maybe she realized what she was getting into."

I shot him a look that could have melted steel.

Finally—finally—after what felt like an eternity but was probably only ten minutes, a janitor appeared with keys. The lock clicked. The doors opened.

And there she was.

The music shifted seamlessly into Shanice Wilson's "Saving Forever For You," and FaLessia appeared at the end of the aisle like an answer to every prayer I'd ever whispered in the dark.

She was radiant—not just beautiful, but luminous. Her dress caught the light from a hundred candles positioned throughout the sanctuary. The ivory fabric seemed to glow against her skin. Her father, Charles Howard, walked beside her with tears already streaming down his face.

But it was her eyes that undid me. She looked at me like I was worth waiting for, worth fighting for, worth choosing every single day for the rest of her life.

The processional music swelled and I felt my own tears starting. Junior stood beside me as my best man, looking uncomfortable in his tuxedo but genuinely happy for me. Pastor Pressley waited at the altar, her face beaming with the joy of someone who had watched me transform from broken boy to whole man.

FaLessia reached the altar, and Mr. Charles placed her hand in mine. He leaned in close and whispered, "Take care of my baby girl."

"With my life," I promised.

The ceremony itself was a blur of beautiful moments. We performed the salt ceremony—an old tradition where bride and groom pour different colored salt into a single vessel. FaLessia's lilac salt and my white salt spiraled together, creating patterns that could never be separated or undone.

"Just like your lives," Pastor Pressley said. "Two distinct individuals becoming one inseparable union."

But it was the vows that broke the congregation.

I had written mine the night before, sitting at my kitchen table, trying to capture everything I felt in words that wouldn't sound ridiculous when spoken aloud. When the moment came, my hands shook as I pulled the paper from my pocket.

"FaLessia," I began, my voice already cracking. "For most of my life, I believed I was unlovable. I believed that people who said they cared would eventually leave. I believed that love was supposed to hurt, that it was supposed to happen in shadows and silence."

I paused, looking into her eyes, seeing my own tears reflected there.

"Then you came along and proved every single one of those beliefs wrong. You loved me when I was broken. You stayed when I was difficult. You saw me—really saw me—and you didn't run away. You taught me that I'm worthy of being loved in the daylight. You showed me that real love doesn't hide, doesn't manipulate, doesn't leave."

The church was silent except for the sound of people crying.

"You're my best friend, my partner, my proof that God keeps His promises. I spent so many years accepting crumbs and calling it a feast. But you—" my voice broke completely, "—you taught me what it feels like to actually sit at the table. To be chosen. To be claimed. To be loved openly and proudly."

I took a shaky breath.

"I promise to spend the rest of my life showing you that you made the right choice. I promise to love you in the light, always. I promise that our children—however God brings them to us—will never wonder if they're wanted. I promise to be the husband you deserve, even on the days when I don't feel like I deserve you. I promise to never stop thanking God for the day He brought you into my life."

Applause broke out before I even finished. People were standing, crying, clapping. Pastor Pressley had to call for order so FaLessia could say her vows.

When she spoke, her voice was steady despite her tears: "Mario, you are the bravest person I know. Not because you survived what you survived, but because you chose to heal. You chose to love again. You chose to trust again. You chose me. And I choose you, today and every day, for the rest of my life."

The kiss was supposed to be brief and tasteful. It wasn't. The congregation erupted again, this time with cheers and whistles that would have made a concert venue proud.

The receiving line brought a moment I'd been dreading: FaLessia meeting Senior for the first time.

He showed up. I honestly didn't think he would—I hadn't exactly rolled out the welcome mat. But there he was, standing in line with everyone else, waiting his turn to congratulate the happy couple.

When he reached us, FaLessia extended her hand with the grace she extends to everyone. "Hello, I'm FaLessia."

He took her hand, his eyes sizing her up the way he'd sized up everything and everyone his whole life—calculating worth, measuring value, determining whether you were useful to him.

"So you're the one who finally got him," he said, his voice carrying that particular tone I knew too well. Not quite hostile, not quite friendly. Just...assessing.

"I'm the blessed one," FaLessia replied smoothly, her hand finding mine. A united front.

The interaction lasted maybe thirty seconds. Pleasantries exchanged. Forced smiles maintained. Then he moved on, and I exhaled for what felt like the first time in minutes.

FaLessia squeezed my hand. "That's him?"

"That's him."

"Okay," she said simply. No judgment, no questions. Just acknowledgment. Later, she would tell me that meeting him helped her understand me better—seeing the source of so much pain put a face to the stories I'd shared. But at that moment, she stood beside me and smiled at the next guest in line.

My father-in-law, Charles Howard—the real father figure in this story—stood nearby, watching the interaction with protective eyes. When Senior walked away, Charles caught my eye and gave me a small nod. *I got you,* that nod said. *You're my son now.*

The Booker family made their presence known in other ways. Some set up a drinking area in the church parking lot—coolers of beer strategically positioned between cars, red Solo cups scattered like confetti. My uncle was already slurring his words during the receiving line.

There were disagreements too. FaLessia's mother and I had gone rounds about the menu. She wanted fried chicken. I wanted baked. The debate stretched over weeks—calls, compromises offered and rejected, tension building with each conversation. In the end, she won decisively.

"I'm paying for the caterer," she reminded me during our final menu discussion, her tone leaving no room for negotiation.

Fried chicken it was. And she made sure I never forgot who had the final say.

During the reception, Juliet Minard—one of FaLessia's coworkers who'd had too much champagne—accidentally kicked one of FaLessia's relatives while attempting some ambitious dance move. They went down hard, and for a moment, I thought we were going to have a brawl at my wedding reception.

But none of it—none of the chaos or drama or family dysfunction—could diminish the joy of that day.

The cakes were perfect. Two three-tiered masterpieces—hers traditional white cake with buttercream, mine a decadent chocolate creation that made my sweet tooth sing. The chocolate-dipped strawberries I fed her were the same ones I'd bought from the farmer's market the day I bought her ring.

When we left the reception, rose petals flying through the air like pink and white snow, FaLessia turned to me and said, "We did it. We're married."

"Against all odds," I replied.

"No," she corrected, squeezing my hand. "Because of God's grace."

She was right, as usual.

I married my best friend on one of the longest nights of the year. Every day since has been nothing but light.

The Children Who Grew in Our Hearts

The river rushes past, relentless and patient at once, and I think about the years of trying to conceive. Month after month of hope and disappointment. Tests and tears and prayers that seemed to go unanswered.

FaLessia's cousin called one day, her voice harsh: "Do you want it?"

It. A baby she was carrying that she didn't want. For months, we prepared our hearts and home for Arlington Booker. We chose his name. We bought clothes and furniture. We let ourselves dream.

Then she changed her mind.

Arlington died in her care months later. The *what-ifs* still haunt me sometimes—could we have saved him? Would he be running through our house right now, playing with his brothers?

But God's plans are not our plans. His ways are higher than our ways.

Jace Alexander and Jaiden Amari Booker didn't grow in FaLessia's womb, but they grew in our hearts long before we ever held them. The day the adoption was finalized, the day the judge declared them legally and permanently ours, I wept like I hadn't wept since the night I gave my life to Christ.

Two boys. Twin sons. A double portion of blessing. They call me Daddy, and every time they say it, something broken in me heals a little more.

I get to break the cycle. I get to show them what a father's love looks like without fists, without fear, without chains in basements. I get to tuck them in at night and tell them they're valued, they're wanted, they're enough exactly as they are.

They will never wonder if they're loved. They will never question their worth. They will never be anyone's punching bag.

The generational curse ends with me.

Education Against All Odds

A family sets up a picnic nearby, their laughter punctuating the sound of the falls. I watch them for a moment, then turn back to the water, thinking about another battle I fought and won.

ITT Tech closed three semesters before I could complete my Bachelor of Applied Science. I was heartbroken. All that work, all that momentum, suddenly gone. But God made a way.

American Business and Technology University accepted me, but ITT had drained my financial aid. We had to self-pay. FaLessia was bringing in most of the income as a newly married couple, but she never once made me feel like my education was a burden.

"You're going to finish," she told me. "We'll figure it out."

And we did. Through sacrifice and faith and her unwavering belief in me, I earned my Bachelor's in Information Systems Engineering and Cybersecurity.

But God wasn't done. Northcentral University accepted me into their master's program. Then, impossibly, a Ph.D. program in Information Technology, specializing in Digital and Networking Forensics.

Doctor Mario DeSean Booker.

The boy who was told he'd never amount to anything. The child beaten for getting a "B." The teenager who slept on floors because no one wanted him. That boy became Dr. Booker.

It almost didn't happen. I lost financial aid again. Nearly got dropped from the program. Faced obstacle after obstacle that would have been perfectly reasonable reasons to quit.

But years earlier, Pastor Betty Pressley had given me a prophecy: "God will see you through college."

And true to His Word, He did exactly that.

Every diploma hanging on my wall is a middle finger to everyone who said I was worthless. Every "Dr. Booker" I hear is proof that their words were lies. Every lecture I give, every student I mentor, every research paper I publish is evidence that I am more than my trauma.

I am the phoenix that rose from ashes they were certain would consume me.

The wind shifts, carrying the mist from the falls across my face. I close my eyes and remember the night God called me to ministry.

I ran.

I listened to the noise of the world, to the whispers of "family" who questioned my worthiness. *Am I lovable? Am I worthy?* Two questions that have haunted me since childhood, two lies that God Himself had to personally dismantle.

He gave me a Scripture that changed everything: Acts 10:15—"And the voice spake unto him again the second time, What God hath cleansed, that call not thou common."

What God has cleansed—me, the broken boy with the scarred back and shattered childhood—is not common. Is not unworthy. Is not too damaged to be used for His purposes.

I am cleansed. I am called. I am CHOSEN.

The ministry I avoided for so long has become the ministry I now embrace. Not because I'm perfect—I'm not. Not because I have totally clean hands—I don't. But because God doesn't call the qualified; He qualifies the called.

The Letter From Dr. Reed

A few months ago, I felt the familiar pull to return to Dr. Reed's office. Life had been good—great, even—but I wanted to share with her how everything had unfolded. The professional success, the marriage thriving, the boys growing, the ministry taking shape. I wanted her to see the fruit of all those painful sessions, all that excavation of trauma, all that rebuilding.

I wanted to say thank you.

I pulled into the familiar parking lot, noting how the office building looked exactly the same. The same sleek windows inviting light into every corner. The same burgundy leather furniture in the waiting room. The same abstract art on the walls—swirls of dark blues and blacks giving way to brilliant golds and whites, storms breaking into dawn.

But when I approached the reception desk, an unfamiliar face looked up at me.

"Can I help you?"

"Yes, I'm here to see Dr. Reed. I know I don't have an appointment, but I was hoping she might have time to—"

"Dr. Reed?" The receptionist's fingers flew across her keyboard. "I'm sorry, but Dr. Reed is no longer with this practice."

The words hit me like a physical blow. "What? When did she leave?"

"It looks like about three months ago." She clicked through a few more screens. "There's a note here that says her work was complete."

Her work was complete.

I stood there, stunned. Dr. Reed had been a constant in my life for years—the one person who knew every dark corner of my story, who had walked with me through the excavation of my deepest wounds. And now she was just...gone?

"Is there a forwarding address? A phone number?"

The receptionist shook her head sympathetically. "I'm sorry. But there is something." She reached into a drawer and pulled out an envelope with my name written in elegant script across the front. "She left this for you."

My hands trembled as I took the envelope. I walked back to my car before opening it, needing privacy for whatever message it contained.

Inside was a single card—no long letter, no explanation, no goodbye. Just a Scripture reference written in that same elegant hand:

Romans 8:31

I pulled out my phone and looked it up, though somewhere deep in my memory, I already knew what it said:

"What shall we then say to these things? If God be for us, who can be against us?"

I sat in my car in that parking lot, tears streaming down my face, understanding flooding through me like light through a broken dam.

Dr. Reed had appeared in my life exactly when I needed her. She had been the safe space, the skilled guide, the steady presence that helped me navigate the labyrinth of my trauma. She had given me tools, shown me truths, held space for my pain until I was strong enough to hold it myself.

And now, her work was complete.

She had left as mysteriously as she had appeared—no dramatic goodbye, no final session, no closure in the traditional sense. Just a Scripture that said everything that needed to be said.

If God be for us, who can be against us?

Not Senior. Not the family that rejected me. Not the lies or the betrayals or the wounds that once seemed too deep to heal. None of it could stand against the God who had orchestrated my restoration.

I can't help but wonder now, sitting here at Stepping Stone Falls with the water rushing past and the seagulls crying overhead—was Dr. Reed even real in the conventional sense? Or was she an angel, a divine appointment, a tool in God's hands sent to help rebuild what the enemy had tried to destroy?

I don't know. I'll probably never know.

But I know this: she came when I needed her. She stayed until her work was done. And she left me with everything I needed to continue the journey without her.

If God be for us, who can be against us?

No one. Nothing. Not even the memories that once held me captive.

Dr. Reed's work was complete. And in a way I'm only beginning to understand, so was mine.

The healing would continue—healing is a lifelong journey, not a destination. But the foundation had been laid. The tools had been given. The truth had been spoken over my life.

I was free to build now. Free to love. Free to live.

Free to be the man God always intended me to be.

The picnic family nearby erupts in laughter, and the sound pierces through me like a knife. *Family.* The word itself has become a weapon wielded against me for decades.

I am the stain on the family tree. The black sheep. The one whose name is spoken with side-eye glances and knowing looks. The person almost everyone loves to hate, and I've spent countless hours with Dr. Reed trying to understand why.

Even now, standing here at these falls, I can feel the weight of their collective rejection pressing down on my shoulders like gravity itself has turned against me.

My maternal grandmother died years ago, but her legacy of division lives on with supernatural persistence. Not to speak ill of the dead—but the dead keep speaking ill of me through the mouths of those who survived her.

The stories I hear about what she said about me, whispered at family gatherings I'm not invited to reaffirm what I've always known: she despised me. I don't know what I did to earn that hatred. *Was I too dark? Too sensitive? Too much like my father? Too much myself?*

She sowed division between the Bookers and the rest of the family with the precision of a master gardener planting seeds of discord. She pitted cousin against cousin, sibling against sibling, creating factions and alliances that persist a decade after her death.

My mother loved her anyway. Worshipped her, even. Sought her approval like water in a desert, never quite getting enough to quench the thirst. I never understood that—especially given how Grandma treated Mama and her children. The favoritism was blatant. The cruelty was casual. But Mama kept coming back for more; kept hoping that this time would be different, that this time she'd finally be enough.

She never was. Neither was I.

But the worst part? A decade after Grandma's death, the lies are still gaining momentum, spreading like cancer through the family tree. And her youngest daughter—my aunt—has become the chief propagator of the propaganda.

She tells anyone who will listen how terribly I treated her. How I abandoned the family. How I think I'm better than everyone else now with my degrees and my success. How I turned my back on blood.

What she conveniently omits from these carefully edited narratives:

When she was diagnosed with cancer, I cooked for her. Week after week, I prepared meals and delivered them to her house because she was too weak to stand at the stove. I showed up with containers of homemade soup, with casseroles, with anything I thought might tempt her appetite.

I took my boys to see her, even though every visit meant walking into a house filled with family members who looked at me with barely concealed contempt. I wanted my sons to know their great-grandmother. I wanted to do the right thing, to be the bigger person, to extend the grace I'd been shown by God.

I tried to push past the history, to build something new on the ashes of the old dysfunction.

Little did I know that while I was extending olive branches, others in the family were setting them on fire behind my back.

The offenses stack up like cordwood:

The side eyes at family gatherings. Every Christmas, every funeral, every reunion where I dare to show my face. The looks that say, "What are you doing here?" The whispers that stop when I enter a room. The conversations that shift when I approach. I learned to read those signals the way sailors read storm clouds.

Befriending my abuser. This one cuts the deepest. Family members who know—who KNOW—what Senior did to me, who saw the bruises, who heard the screams, who witnessed the aftermath. And yet, they maintain relationships with him. They invite him to their homes. They laugh at his jokes. They celebrate his birthdays.

When I confronted one cousin about it, she said, "Well, that's between you and him. I can still have my own relationship with Uncle Mike."

As if abuse exists in a vacuum. As if remaining friendly with my tormentor isn't a choice that speaks volumes about whose side you're on.

Not inviting me to family functions. I find out about weddings on Facebook. I learn about birthday parties through other people's Instagram stories. Family reunions happen, and I discover them after the fact through posted photos where everyone looks so happy, so unified, so complete without me.

Sometimes I wonder if they even notice I'm missing. Sometimes I think that's exactly the point.

Weaponizing my abusive past. This is the cruelest cut of all. When I dare to speak up, when I dare to set boundaries, when I dare to say "no" to dysfunction, they use my trauma against me.

"You're too sensitive because of what happened to you."

"You need to get over the past."

"Not everything is about your childhood, Mario."

They take the most vulnerable, broken parts of my story and turn them into character flaws. They pathologize my healing as if wanting to be treated with basic human dignity is somehow unreasonable.

Using cousins to spread lies. The younger generation, who weren't even alive during my childhood, have been fed a steady diet of misinformation about who I am and what I've done. They believe the lies because they've never heard my side. They've been inoculated against me before we even met.

I've watched cousins I used to play with as a child grow up and have children of their own, children who will be taught the same lies, who will continue the cycle of rejection into the next generation.

The poison keeps spreading.

Dr. Reed reminded me of Luke 21:16: "And ye shall be betrayed both by parents, and brethren, and kinsfolks, and friends; and some of you shall they cause to be put to death."

Jesus Himself warned that family would betray us. That blood wouldn't protect us from hurt. That sometimes the people who share our DNA would be the ones holding the knife.

But the verse doesn't end there. Verse 18 promises: "But there shall not an hair of your head perish."

They can betray me, but they cannot destroy me.

She also pointed me to Matthew 12:48-50, where Jesus redefines family entirely: "...Who is my mother? and who are my brethren? And he stretched forth his hand toward his disciples, and said, Behold my mother and my brethren! For whosoever shall do the will of my Father which is in heaven, the same is my brother, and sister, and mother."

My family isn't defined by the blood that betrays me. It's defined by the covenant that keeps me.

The Ormonds can have their reunions, their inside jokes, their shared history that conveniently edits me out of the narrative. They can keep their lies and their selective memories and their collective decision that I'm not worth knowing.

I have a different family now. A chosen family. A family that chose me back.

And that makes all the difference.

I walk down the path at Stepping Stone Falls, and my shadow walks beside me—but it's not alone. In my mind's eye, I see other shadows: FaLessia's, Jaiden's, Jace's. My chosen family. My covenant family.

God blessed me with a new family when the old one rejected me. He gave me new hope when the past tried to define my future. He offers new mercy every morning when yesterday's wounds try to reopen.

I think about my boys at home, probably playing video games or arguing about whose turn it is to pick the movie. I think about FaLessia, likely preparing dinner and wondering when I'll be home from my walk. I think about my church family who celebrates my victories and prays through my struggles.

I think about Dr. Reed, who helped me excavate the trauma and rebuild on solid ground.

I think about my students, who call me Dr. Booker and don't know that every time they do, they're speaking life into wounds they can't see.

I am not the boy in the basement anymore.

I am not the teenager sleeping on floors.

I am not the young man accepting crumbs and calling it love.

I am Dr. Mario DeSean Booker—husband, father, minister, professor, survivor, thriver.

I am proof that what the enemy meant for evil, God used for good.

I am evidence that chains can be broken, that cycles can end, that phoenixes really do rise.

Moving Forward

The sun is setting now, painting the sky in shades of purple and gold—my wedding colors, I realize with a smile. The water continues its ancient work, smoothing stones, carving paths, flowing relentlessly toward its destination.

I am like this river. Shaped by the rocks I've flowed over, persistent despite obstacles, always moving forward.

My shadow stretches even longer now in the fading light, but I'm not afraid of it anymore. Shadows only exist where light shines. For so long, I lived in complete darkness where even shadows couldn't form. Now I stand in the light, and yes, there's a shadow—but that shadow proves the light is real.

God walks with me. Even when I can't feel Him, even when family betrays me, even when old wounds try to reopen—He's there. My shadow is proof. My survival is proof. My success is proof.

I know who holds tomorrow. And because I know Him, I can release yesterday.

The family reunion nearby is packing up now, loading cars and hugging goodbye. I watch them for a moment, feeling the old ache of not belonging, but also feeling something new: contentment with the family I've been given.

I pull out my phone and text FaLessia: *"On my way home. Love you."*

Her response comes immediately: *"The boys want tacos. Can you stop and grab shells? Love you more."*

Simple. Ordinary. Beautiful.

This is what I fought for. This is what I survived for. Not the extraordinary moments, but the ordinary ones—taco shells and homework help and bedtime stories. The quiet accumulation of days spent being loved and giving love in return.

As I walk back to my car, I notice something I've never seen before: actual stepping stones placed deliberately across a shallow part of the river. They're worn smooth by countless feet, each one a small island of stability in the current.

That's what my journey has been—stepping stones placed by God across the raging waters of my past. Dr. Reed. FaLessia. My education. My faith. My children. Each one a place to stand, a way to cross over from death to life.

I didn't walk on water. I used the stones God provided.

And now I'm on the other side.

I get in my car and head home to my family—not the one that rejected me, but the one that chose me. The one that stays. The one that loves me in the light.

Behind me, the falls continue their eternal cascade, water rushing over stone, smoothing rough edges, carving beauty from resistance.

Just like God did with me.

Against all odds, this is my unbroken story.

And it's just beginning.

About the Author

Dr. Mario DeSean Booker is a leading voice at the intersection of technology and social justice. As a Full-Time Professor of Graduate Information Technology at Purdue University Global, he holds a Ph.D. in Information Technology with a concentration in Digital Forensics and dedicates his research to challenging algorithmic discrimination and digital colonialism. His 2025 book, *404: Justice Not Found*, frames his mission to ensure technology serves democratic governance. A prolific author, Dr. Booker also released *Once Upon A Quantum* in 2025.

Beyond his academic and industry expertise, Dr. Booker is an active community advocate, having served on the Flint Community Advisory Taskforce for Public Safety. He also serves as an ordained minister at HOPE Ministries. Above all, he is a family man, who cherishes his time with his wife of 20 years, FaLessia, and their sons Jaiden and Jace. His life's work is a testament to his belief that technological inquiry and social justice are mutually reinforcing endeavors.

However, Dr. Booker has another side...

As the "Doctor of Drama," Mario DeSean Booker pens the "Tried in Fire" book series. The first three books in that series, *Beauty for Ashes, No Ordinary First Lady,* and *I Who Have Nothing* were released to enthusiastic early reader praise. Dr. Booker is currently writing the fourth book in the series.

www.ingramcontent.com/pod-product-compliance
Lightning Source LLC
Chambersburg PA
CBHW071739150726
47998CB00005B/1723